THE LADY IN CEMENT

THE LADY IN CEMENT

TONY ROME

The Trilogy   Book Two

MARVIN H. ALBERT

THE LADY IN CEMENT
TONY ROME
The Trilogy
Book Two

This unabridged 2025 edition of *The Lady in Cement* is printed in arrangement with the estate of author Marvin H. Albert by Compass Rose Publishing
228 Park Ave. S #620056
New York, NY. 10003-1502

Softcover ISBN: 979-8-9988995-4-6

Front cover photo: Joseph Etchingham
Back cover photo: Simon Kuznetsov
Author sketch: Estate of author Marvin H. Albert

Cover Design by: Danielle Kane and Thomas Hurd

Publisher's Note: The Tony Rome series of three novels was originally published between 1960 and 1962. They are set in that time period and reflect the attitudes of the time. The publisher's decision to keep the text true to the author's vision is not meant in any way to endorse offensive cultural representations or language.

CAST OF CHARACTERS

Anthony Rome—A poker-playing, brandy-drinking private eye, he gambled with danger in a setting of sun, sin and sand, and found himself in a game with the ace of death high.

Art Santini—A short, plump police lieutenant with dark, liquid eyes and a deceptive blandness, his Miami rogues' gallery was useless without Rome's memory for a face.

Maria Barreto—A saucy stripper with jet-black hair and a strangely innocent look, the curvaceous Cuban sought a haven in Miami Beach, but her luck ran out when she chose a roommate.

Larry Score—A two-timing, double-crossing gunman, he had the pretty-boy features of a matinee idol, enough to make him a lady-killer—and a mankiller, too.

Danny Yale—A stocky, hard-faced man with slick dark hair and mean, piercing eyes, the smooth operator of the Frenzy Club passed up B-girls for bigger game.

Kit Forrest—A green-eyed, high-spirited lass with roan-colored hair and fine-boned features, Gretchen's younger sister played a hunch, and for once the odds were with her.

Gretchen Forrest—A brassy, brazen, much-married millionheiress whose gems and gigolos blazed a glittering trail through Miami Beach, she bought her way out of every jam, until the stakes were over her head.

CAST OF CHARACTERS

Al Mungo——A balding "retired" mobster with a murderous gash for a mouth, his goal was high society, but the means he used were low.

Shev——A heavyweight hood with a welterweight frame, the former boxer came out punching every time Mungo rang the bell.

Frenchy——A brawny thug with the face of a good-natured ape, Mungo's pet football tackle was on the offense——and the opposition didn't scare him.

Paul Mungo——A sullen, spoiled young man with a go-to-hell slouch, Mungo's son ignored his father's side kicks, but not his father's women.

Earl Gronsky——A bearlike bruiser with a wolfish grin, the "Mad Russian" could wield a knife, and he liked to carve initials——in most peculiar places.

Arnie Sherwin——A fat, down-and-out caricaturist with a shaved skull and defiant beard, the self-styled beatnik was a paid guest at gala gatherings——and he always remembered the faces he drew.

"ANTHONY ROME?"

It was a man's voice, blurred as though he had a handkerchief over the mouthpiece. "I read in the paper about you findin' the dame in the water just before the sharks hit."

Something in his smart tone got me mad. "So what's it to you?"

"So you were the only one who saw her face." His voice went on softly. "I got some friendly advice—forget what she looked like."

"For how much?"

"We got more wet cement. You'd be alive when you went in. Nothing to breathe but water—lots of it!"

1.

I WAS THIRTY FEET UNDER THE SURFACE of the ocean when I first saw the naked woman standing on the bottom below me.

It was shortly after dawn. I was skin-diving toward a submerged coral reef between Key Biscayne and Fowey Rocks, wearing my aqualung, face mask and fins, with a lead weighted canvas belt buckled over my swimming trunks. The woman below me wore no diving outfit. She wore nothing.

The water was a brilliant, clear turquoise. I could see her distinctly. Her face was tilted up toward me, her eyes staring with a frozen wildness, her water-filled mouth strained wide open as though she were screaming at me.

I checked my downward glide, stared at her through the glass of my mask, forcing myself to continue breathing slowly through the mouthpiece clamped between my teeth. The water, which had felt so pleasantly warm when I first plunged into it, seemed suddenly to hold a clammy chill that made my skin crawl.

She stood in a narrow depression in the coral a few feet from the jagged seaward slope of the reef that plunged into the murky blackness of five-hundred-foot depths. She was young, with a ripe-curved figure. But for the grimace of terror contorting her face, she might have been pretty.

Her nude body swung to and fro in the heavy ground swell—

her full young breasts swaying, her stiffly outflung arms waving at me, her long blond hair streaming upward.

But despite the strong tug of the current, she remained standing where she was. Propelling myself reluctantly closer with a short flutter kick, I saw why.

Her feet were encased in a solid square block of cement.

Cold fingers squeezed my brain. I had a sense of unreality. But I knew that girl standing in the block of hardened cement below me was real. As real as the vivid red, yellow and violet mat sponges plastered to the reef. As real as the purple lace sea fans and the multibranched elkhorn coral formations among which she stood.

I wasn't down deep enough or long enough to be experiencing one of the weird visions that sometimes accompany nitrogen narcosis—the insidious "rapture of the deep." It was my first dive of the morning. I'd sailed out from Miami before dawn in my boat, the *Straight Pass,* together with my friend Jack McComb, a charter-boat captain who'd lost a leg in the war. We were stealing a day's holiday from our respective jobs to engage in a favorite southern-Florida pursuit—hunting sunken treasure wrecks. Somewhere between Key Biscayne and Fowey Rocks—according to the history books—eleven overloaded Spanish treasure galleons had gone down in a 1591 hurricane.

At dawn I'd won the flip of a coin and taken the first turn at diving while McComb stayed topside to handle my boat. I'd plunged downward into the ocean seeking the legendary sunken treasure—and discovered instead this hideous underwater horror straight out of a cold-sweat nightmare.

It wasn't the first violently dead body I'd ever come upon.

A private detective in Florida has to develop a certain amount of emotional armor or get out of the business. But I wasn't prepared to find it out there, under the sea, where I sought escape from the unpleasant realities of what people were capable of doing to each other.

So it took me longer than usual to recover from the first shock. When I did, I began swimming down to her. As I drew closer, I saw the small open wound in her body, just below the breastbone.

And I saw something else. Something I should have noticed before that. There were no fish around.

Ordinarily, the nooks and crannies of a submerged reef are infested with small fish of all kinds in those warm waters. They should have been swarming all around the dead girl. But there were none.

I realized it at the same instant that I saw the reason. It glided slowly into view from behind a coral boulder on the other side of the woman standing in the cement block—a sleek, massive, fifteen-foot white shark.

I twisted to an abrupt underwater halt, my heart thudding sickeningly.

There are sharks and sharks. Most are nothing to be afraid of. The dusky shark most often found in Florida waters isn't interested in eating anything other than small, helpless fishes. It is extremely timid, and will flee at the first sign of boldness on a man's part.

The white shark is a different matter. Its scientific name is *Carcharodon carcharias*—and it can finish you before you finish pronouncing that. The white shark is a man-eater, a savage fighter with a voracious appetite.

I watched, frozen, as this one thrust its massive bulk fully into view with a negligent flip of its caudal fin. It slipped like oil through the water in my direction, then turned and began slowly circling the woman inquisitively, ignoring me.

I sucked in air through the mouthpiece attached to the tank strapped on my back. Began to shake off the paralyzing grip of fear. Then I glimpsed a moving shadow off to my left. I twisted toward it.

Another man-eating white shark was gliding straight toward me.

It stopped when I spun to face it. It hovered there twenty feet from me, watching. Its snout seemed aimed at me, its gill slits working and its long gash of a mouth looking big enough to drive a car into.

My right hand closed around the cork handle of my float knife. I drew it from the belt. As a weapon, a knife was about as much use against a white shark as a hatpin would be against a lion. Driving the knife in deep wasn't likely to do effective damage, and would succeed only in angering the monster. But sometimes a light jab with the point of a knife would make a shark decide to leave you alone.

All sharks are unpredictable, including white sharks. It depended on whether these two were hungry. If they weren't, I might be able to drive them off. If they were, they'd try to make a meal of me.

Below and off to my right, the first shark suddenly decided that the naked woman it was circling was harmless. It flashed in on her. For a split second it seemed to pause with its face touching hers, as though it were kissing her in passing. Then its obscuring body flashed on, and I could see the woman again.

The shark's monstrous gash of a mouth, armed with razor-sharp teeth, had scooped away most of her face.

Nausea rose in my throat, interfering with my regular air intake through the mouthpiece. I fought it down, looked at the second shark. It was still there, watching me.

I had to do something. Right away. Fluttering my rubber fins, I started through the water.

The shark that had picked me made up its mind abruptly. It flicked its tail and came after me like a jet-propelled sub.

I abandoned my upward movement and desperately began thrashing my arms and legs to scare it off. It kept coming, looming immense as it closed in on me. I blew hard into my mouthpiece, sending out a burst of air bubbles from my breathing apparatus to join the splashing of my arms and legs. And prayed.

The shark swerved just as it reached me. Its long white belly rushed past my side by inches. I saw its mouth open—and all those jagged, pointed teeth. I thought I felt the tip of one fin brush my hip.

I jerked around to keep facing it. The shark turned and began circling, its tiny eyes studying me. I kept twisting to prevent its getting behind me. Sparing one swift glance downward, I saw that the other shark was still dealing with the cement-anchored woman. Continuing to turn as the shark circled me, I resumed my slow flutter kick toward the surface. The shark rose with me, its circles tightening closer around me. Above us, the keel of my boat began to loom nearer.

Suddenly, the shark presented its white belly to me again and attacked, its opening mouth aimed for a snatch at my feet. I jerked my knees up to my chest, twisted frantically as the gaping mouth grabbed for me, and jabbed the point of my knife against its snout. The water exploded as the shark spasmed away from the knife and shot past under me.

With one quick movement, I detached the weight belt and let it sink. In almost the same instant, using both arms and legs, I drove myself upward with all my strength.

My head broke the surface, cleared it. But that left me in the worst possible position—my legs and lower body dangling under the water, exposed and unprotected. I doubled my legs up against me again and ducked my face back into the water, peering through my mask. The shark was at the surface, too. It was driving straight for me at fantastic speed. And this time the knife wasn't going to stop it.

The shark was less than ten feet away when its whole body seemed to jolt into some invisible barrier. It swerved to the left. At the same time, a sharp cracking sound reached my ears.

The sound was repeated. The shark jerked around in a tight circle. Its blood began to stain the water it was thrashing to a pink froth. There was a third sharp crack. The shark spun around as though trying to bite itself, then abruptly headed for the bottom, sounding like a whale.

I raised my head above the surface, turned to locate the boat. Jack McComb was perched on his single leg in the cockpit, his left hand braced against the deckhouse overhang, a revolver in his right hand.

Letting my knife float out of my hand, I swam to the boat as fast as I could manage it. Grasping the stern ladder, I dragged myself over the side and into the cockpit. My heart was going like a trip hammer as I spat out the mouthpiece and shut off the air valve. My legs were rubbery.

"Christ almighty!" McComb growled, his tough, dark-weathered face still scared. "The bastard almost got you!"

"Almost," I gasped as I stripped off my mask.

"I saw all the commotion down there. When you and that shark came up near enough for me to see what was up, I got this in a hurry." McComb held up the .38 I kept in the cabin.

"Nice shooting," I told him, from the heart. "The drinks are on me ashore. Enough to get us both stoned." I sucked my lungs full of air, let out my breath slowly. "Right now there's a murdered woman down there we've got to bring up."

McComb blinked. "Huh?"

I nodded. "You heard right. Get me the longest line aboard."

McComb's puzzled frown remained. But he hurried to get what I wanted. Ashore, his missing leg forced him to hobble along on crutches. But in a boat, using handholds to aid him, he was as nimble as any sailor. That was what had sold him on charter-boat fishing after the war.

While McComb got the line, I went for my speargun. It was a compact, gas-powered job, one of the most powerful underwater guns made. It was capable of delivering enough of an impact for even a shark, if my aim was true.

I free-loaded a short spear with a harpoon barb into the gun and returned to the cockpit with it, walking awkwardly in my rubber-finned feet, bent forward to balance the weight of the air tank strapped to my back. McComb was already there with the line. At one end of it he'd fashioned a big slipknot loop. He was looking over the side.

"Look at that," he said softly, nodding at what he was watching. Ten feet down in the ocean, the two sharks were thrashing over and over in a furious death battle, bloody air bubbles rising from them to the disturbed surface.

I felt a tight, vicious grin stretch my lips.

Nothing incites a shark like the scent of fresh-flowing blood. When the shark McComb shot had dived, streaming blood from its wounds, the other shark had obviously abandoned the bloodless corpse of the woman to attack its now vulnerable, juicier ex-partner.

"They deserve each other," I murmured, and spat on my face mask. I rubbed the saliva over the glass to keep my breath from fogging it underwater, pulled the mask on my face.

"You really going back in—with them two?" McComb demanded with a worried frown.

"They're too busy right now to notice me."

"You hope," McComb said dryly.

"I hope," I agreed, and got the mouthpiece between my teeth. I took the noose end of the line from him and slipped my left arm through the loop. Carrying the speargun, I got one leg over the side.

"Tony," McComb said, "you're crazy."

I nodded, swung my other leg over, and went into the ocean.

I went under cautiously, pausing at ten feet to eye the embattled sharks slashing away at each other with those terrible teeth. I continued my descent in a wide downward circle that kept me well away from them. They went on with their private death fight, paying no attention to me. But I didn't ever turn my back on them. And I continued to hold the speargun ready, gripped tightly in my hand, all the way down.

The nude blonde was still on the coral reef, standing in her block of cement. I tried to look at her as little as possible as I got the loop around her. More than her face was missing now. The shark had done ghastly work on her body, gouging away the flesh of one hip and shredding one of her arms. I drew the slipknot tight, securing the loop around her narrow waist. Then I left her and began kicking my way back to the surface.

The shark McComb had plugged three times was by then floating belly up, with the other shark triumphantly tearing out its entrails—too engrossed in what it was doing to be aware of me gliding upward past them. Nevertheless, I went shaky with relief when I finally had the solid deck of the *Straight Pass* under my feet again.

McComb waited, holding the other end of the line. I stripped off the aqualung, mask and fins. Then the two of us began hauling the cement-weighted corpse of the nude blonde up to the surface. McComb had trouble keeping his stomach out of his mouth when he got his first look at her. I'd already seen her, and I had sense enough not to look again. We laid her out by the cockpit transom. I went up the ladder to the flying bridge wheel and got the boat underway immediately, letting wind and sun dry the seawater off me as I headed in.

The *Straight Pass,* a sleek, thirty-six-foot cabin cruiser with twin Chrysler Crown engines, was originally a sports job—and built for speed. After I'd acquired her in a high-stakes crap game, I'd renamed her in honor of the four passes in a row I'd thrown to win her, and refitted her for fishing and as a permanent floating home for me. But I hadn't tampered with her speed.

I used all of that speed getting us back to Miami with our grisly cargo.

2.

MORGUES ARE DEPRESSINGLY ALIKE. What were once God-touched human beings are handled in a way to shake your faith that they were ever anything other than strangely fashioned inanimate slabs of meat and bone. You'll find more respect shown for the merchandise handled in any well-run butcher shop. The Dade County morgue was no exception.

I didn't stay long in the autopsy room. I wouldn't have entered it in the first place, except that Lieutenant Santini, of Miami Homicide, had taken me to have a word with Dr. Flanders, who was doing the autopsy on the blonde I had brought out of the drink.

They'd broken open the cement block that had anchored her feet. All the chunks of cement had been collected neatly in a cardboard box as evidence. The faceless body had been stretched out on the operating table for the necessary task determining as much as possible about her and her death.

The first part wasn't so bad. The exterior examination. Dr. Flanders went over her from head to toe, searching for all outer marks of violence. His running commentary on the woman's corpse was written down by his assistant. Flanders was clinically detailed about what the shark's teeth had done to her face and body, measuring the wounds carefully. The small wound I'd noticed just under her breastbone, the doctor guessed on the basis of purely exterior examination, had been made by a sharp, narrow-bladed knife driven into her in an upward direction. Whether that was what had killed her he couldn't tell till he finished the autopsy.

Flanders went on with the exterior job. The corpse was exactly five feet four inches tall, must have weighed about one hundred and twenty pounds. Hips, about thirty-six inches. Waist, twenty-four inches. Bust, thirty-seven inches. The blond hair was natural. She had a small appendectomy scar; a couple ancient scars on her shins, probably from childhood; a tiny, dark beauty spot behind her left earlobe; silver polish on her nails; no vaccination marks on the arm the shark hadn't mangled.

All of that I stayed through. But when Dr. Flanders picked up a scalpel in one rubber-gloved hand, I tapped Lieutenant Santini on the arm.

"I'll sit out this hand," I told him quietly.

Art Santini was a short, plump man with a deceptively bland, round face. He turned his dark, liquid eyes on me. "Chicken!" he whispered. But he didn't look any healthier than I felt.

I closed the door behind me. I knew exactly what was happening in the room I'd left. I'd seen enough of it back in the days when I'd been a detective on the Miami police force. Her abdomen would be stripped open, her breastbone sawed out, the top of her skull sawed open. Every organ in her body would be taken out, examined, weighed, cut open and examined again. Specimens of organ tissue, blood vessels and any partially digested food found in the intestinal tract would be taken and chemically analyzed. Finally, she'd be reassembled, filed away in one of the cold-storage lockers in the morgue to await identification. If no one claimed her inside a month, she would get a pauper's burial by the county.

I knew all that. That was bad enough. At least I didn't have to watch it being done.

Wishing I'd brought my flask of brandy along, I fished a pack of Luckies out of my dungarees, leaned against the damp corridor wall beside the autopsy-room door and smoked, wondering how

Jack McComb was making out. Since no one knew where the woman I'd found had been murdered, all kinds of law had entered the case—Miami Homicide, the county Metro police, the Florida state cops. There was even an investigator from the Coast Guard, on the possibility that the blonde had been killed on some vessel out at sea. They questioned us separately—me first. When I'd left with Santini for the autopsy room, they'd been taking McComb's statement from him. And not liking it any better than they'd liked mine.

I didn't blame them. We'd brought them a real package of headaches. A murdered woman with no identification and no face to identify her by. It would make front-page headlines and create terrific pressure on the police to come up with an answer. They'd done their best to get a decent set of prints off the fingers of the hand the shark hadn't gotten to. But the blonde had been in the water long enough to give them dependable results.

I was thankful for one thing. No one had as yet suggested McComb and I might have murdered the girl; then tossed her in the ocean, persuaded a shark to mutilate her beyond recognition, and hauled her up again—bringing her corpse back just to confuse the cops. The police are busy, overworked men who prefer the easiest explanations they can find. But even they weren't prepared to go that far to get out from under a lousy case.

I'd had quite a pile of cigarette butts on the linoleum of the corridor floor by the time Lieutenant Santini came out of the autopsy room. He shut the door and leaned sickly against the wall beside me.

"Gimme one of your cigarettes," he rasped.

"Use up all of yours inside there?"

"I stopped smoking a month ago."

I said, "Oh," and shook a Lucky out of the pack for him. When he got it between his teeth, I lit it for him. His hands didn't look any too steady.

I waited till he'd taken a few deep drags, then asked him, "Well?"

"Let's get out of here," he growled. "The bar across the street."

I raised an eyebrow at him. "On duty? You'll never make captain that way."

"Drop dead."

We left through the cold, dank, formaldehyde-scented dampness of the dim-lighted morgue storage chamber, with its rows of corpse-containing lockers. When we emerged from the basement door of the building into the daylight outside, it was like stepping out of a grave. The blazing sunlight hit us, hurting my eyes. Perspiration trickled under my polo shirt by the time we'd crossed the street. It was a relief to get into the murky coolness of the saloon.

We took a back booth. Santini ordered a double bourbon on the rocks. I had a brandy. I sipped my drink and watched him gulp his.

When he'd downed it all, I asked him again, "Well?"

Santini sighed and wiped his gentle mouth with the back of his hand. "She's—she *was*—in her early or middle twenties. She'd had relations with men, but she'd never delivered any babies. That's all we know about her—before she got dead."

He picked up his glass, took one of the melting ice cubes between his teeth and began crunching it up. He swallowed, set the glass back down with a thump and looked at me again.

"She wasn't strangled, shot, poisoned," he intoned. "And she definitely wasn't drowned. She was dead when she went into the drink. Hardly any water in her lungs. That knife wound killed her. A narrow, long blade. It was driven in under her breastbone and up into her heart. Then it was pulled out of her. She must've died within seconds."

"When?"

Santini shrugged. "Flanders wouldn't be definite. He made a guess at somewhere between ten and twenty hours before you fished her out. But it's only a guess."

"How long was she in the water?"

Santini eyed me. "Not more than an hour, certainly. Maybe half an hour. Possibly less."

"I found her at first light this morning. She must've been dumped just before dawn."

"How long was your boat at that spot before you dove?"

"About five minutes."

He pursed his lips. "That shaves it mighty close. Whoever did it must've dropped her and sailed away just before your boat came in sight. You didn't see any other boat?"

I shook my head.

"Swell," he muttered unhappily. He stood up. "Well, let's go back to my office."

"You've already taken my statement,'* I said. "It hasn't changed."

"We haven't got anything identifying this dame," Santini pointed out. "You're the only one saw what she looked like before that shark ruined her face. You've got a big day of work ahead."

I resigned myself to it. We went back to Santini's office. They had let McComb go shortly after we arrived. But I stayed. For the next three hours I went through women's photographs from the missing-persons files of the Miami department, the state cops and the local office of the FBI.

It wasn't easy to decide as I examined picture after picture. I'd only gotten that one short look at her death-distorted face—and underwater, at that. If it hadn't been for my police training, there were several photos that I might have picked, but in the end, I rejected them all.

As I slipped the last photo back in its envelope, Santini looked up at me over the rim of the cardboard container from which he was drinking some tepid coffee. We'd killed six containers of the stuff between us.

"Nothing?" he suggested hopelessly.

"Nope."

He considered the pile of envelopes and missing-persons books on the desk between us. "You might as well scram, Tony. We've got your description of the lady's face. Such as it is."

I stood up. "Don't start calling me over here every time some blonde runs out on her husband. I've got more things to do with my time than—"

"Sure you have," Santini stated. "Like hunting for sunken treasure." He made a face. "What in hell kind of way is that for a grown man to spend his time?"

I grinned at him. "I'm still a boy. What I want to be when I grow up is rich."

"What good would it do you? You'd only blow it all in some sudden-death poker game."

I acknowledged the truth of that. But my mind wasn't on our conversation. "When the story about finding that blonde comes out in the papers," I mused, "you'll be swamped with cranks claiming to know who she is.

"The radio broadcasts were carrying the story an hour after you brought her in. We've already had a dozen of those calls. We're going to have a grand time, checking them all down. You really did us a favor, bringing her in like that."

"It wasn't exactly fun," I murmured, and went to the door of his office. I opened it, paused and glanced back at Santini. "Just a thought, Art. This business about sinking her with a cement block hardened around her feet. That's an old mobster bit. And some of those old-timers don't know it's gone out of style."

Santini nodded. "I know. You got any particular mobster in mind?"

I shrugged. "This being the season here in Miami, you've got a lot to choose from." I went out, shutting the door quietly behind me.

Outside the building, the sunlight blinded me again. I strolled to the corner newsstand, squinting while my eyes adjusted to the glare. The early-afternoon edition of the papers had already hit the streets with the story on the front page. There was a two-column picture with it. An artist's sketch of a blond woman. There was a dark question mark where her face should have been. The story was substantially correct. McComb and I got a big play, which wouldn't hurt business for either of us. The story made the point that I was the only one who had seen the blonde's face before the shark destroyed it.

I stood there beside the newsstand and thought about an unknown person reading that. A person capable of stabbing a woman to death expertly, then encasing her feet in cement and taking her out to sea for a quiet water burial.

Whoever had done it had made a slight mistake in figuring his—or her—position. A few feet farther out, and the body would have sunk to the bottom under five hundred feet of ocean; no trace of it would ever have been found.

I looked at the picture with the question-mark face some more, remembering what her face had looked like when I'd first seen her. Finally, I gave the paper back to the news dealer and went away from there.

But the memory of her face—her eyes staring wildly and her open mouth screaming something at me through the depths of the sea—*that* wouldn't go away.

I took the *Straight Pass* out of the municipal docks and sailed her down to my home berth at Dinner Key. McComb had already taken a cab there. He kept his charter-fishing boat moored at the same pier as mine. Like me, he lived aboard. I found him there waiting. For a time, we talked about what had happened. But between us we couldn't come up with any conclusions other than that it had been one of the worst days either of us had ever spent out on the water.

That night McComb swung up the pier on his crutches to my boat, and I kept my promise about supplying the drinks. But neither of us was really in a mood to get stoned. Instead, we played two-handed stud with chips for our shares of the sunken treasure we'd someday find. The white chips represented bars of silver; the red chips were for gold bars; the blue chips stood for precious gems.

Tangerine, a rangy, battle-damaged tomcat with a chewed-off ear who bummed around the waterfront, prowled aboard off the pier and growled for a handout. After lapping up the saucer of milk

I put down for him, he sat back for a while and watched us play. His yellow eyes darted back and forth following the flash of the cards. I wished I had Tangerine's poker face. I tried twice to scare McComb out with a bluff hand. Both times McComb shrewdly let me sweeten the pot and then called me.

McComb had won about a quarter of a million dollars' worth of my share of Spanish treasure when the phone I had hooked into the dock line rang up on the flying bridge.

I went up the ladder, lifted the phone and said, "Yeah?"

"Anthony Rome?" It was a man's voice, blurred as though he'd drawn a handkerchief taut over the mouthpiece.

"Who's this?"

I read in the paper about you being the only one saw the dame's face, his voice said softly into my ear. "I got some friendly advice. Just forget what she looked like."

"For how much?" I asked quietly. The flesh of my face seemed suddenly to have become too tight.

"We got more wet cement," he went on unemotionally. "You'd be alive when you went in. It's a lousy way to die—with nothing to breathe but water."

"Let's meet somewhere," I said, trying to keep the tightness out of my voice, "and talk it over."

"We've talked. Just forget what she looked like. It's no business of yours. You got nothing to gain. You got your life to lose. We know how to get you any time we want you. It'd be no trouble at all."

The line went dead.

3.

I STOOD THERE FOR A MOMENT STARING out at the moonlight shimmering on the dark surface of the ocean. Then I hung up and went back down to the deckhouse.

McComb looked at my face as I sat down. "Business or pleasure?"

"Just a crank," I told him. We resumed the playing.

But later that night, after I opened the cabin settee, which converted into a double bed, I got out the .38 Police Special and reloaded it. I slept with it on the mattress close to my hand. I didn't sleep well.

And the next morning, when I drove up to my office in Miami, I was wearing the gun in a belt holster under the jacket of my lightweight suit.

I didn't get to spend much of that day in my office. I'd cleared up my last case—the locating of a missing heir—on Monday. No new business had come in on Tuesday, and McComb wanted a little relief from taking inept fishermen out on the Gulf Stream, which was why we'd decided to spend Wednesday out at sea, diving for a highly improbable treasure.

That Thursday morning started out busily enough. There was a dowdy, middle-aged woman waiting for me when I got to my office. She wanted me to find out if her son's wife was cheating on him. I wasn't that hungry. I told her my fee was a thousand dollars a day for breaking up young marriages. She promised to report me to the Better Business Bureau, and stalked out.

A few minutes later a young man came in. He turned out to be a reporter who wanted a first-person story from me for his paper on how I'd found the blonde in the ocean. I gave it to him. That kind of publicity was bound to inject more financial life into my business. But when he asked for a picture of me, I thought about the unknown man who phoned the warning the previous night. He might or might not know exactly what I looked like. There was no sense making it easy for them to get me. I told the reporter I had no photos of myself, and declined to be photographed at his newspaper's studio.

Ten minutes after he left, Lieutenant Santini was on the phone. Headquarters had seven new <u>mis</u>sing women's pictures for me to look at.

I drove over and looked at them. None were of the blonde I'd found. I left Headquarters feeling savagely restless, in no mood to return to the office. I decided to let off steam at the Hialeah Park race track.

I played most of the races hard-headedly, sticking with the favorites and near-favorites. I won some, but lost more.

By the end of the next-to-last race, I was eighty-two dollars that I couldn't afford in the hole.

So after spending ten minutes doping the last race, I decided to hell with being smart, and bet fifty dollars on a long shot named Silly Boy to win. I knew better. And it left me five dollars and change in my pocket and some two hundred in the bank. But playing an occasional dark horse was a gambler's perversion I couldn't break.

This time my luck was running. Silly Boy went crazy and pounded over the finish line a nose ahead of a streak of lightning that he didn't have any business being on the same track with.

At odds of twenty-to-one. Which earned me a neat one thousand dollars on my fifty-buck investment. It made me feel a lot better about all the days and dollars I'd wasted at the track that month.

I pocketed my winnings and left the betting window in a jubilant frame of mind. But the good feeling was dampened a bit by a call to my office. Margo, secretary to the lawyer in the next office to mine, took my calls on an extension phone when I wasn't there. She told me Lieutenant Santini wanted me to come to his office and look at another photograph.

I sighed irritably as I went to my car. This sort of thing was likely to continue for a long time.

Santini wasn't in when I got to Headquarters. He'd gone off duty half an hour before. But he'd left a photograph for me and word to phone him after I looked at it. It was an eight-by-ten glossy, a full-face glamour photograph of a blonde.

The girl in the picture was about the right age, pretty in a hard way, and the bright blond hair was long enough. But the total impression was quite different from what I remembered of the girl I'd found under the sea.

But something got to me. I took another, more careful look, trying to ignore her expression of phony sensuality, the excess of make-up and the false eyelashes, the passionately narrowed eyes, the pouting of the lips.

The girl in the photo had the same long, straight nose as the blonde I'd found. The arch of the plucked eyebrows was the same. I studied the structure of her cheeks, her jawline. The longer I looked, the less sure I became of my first impression. Finally, I phoned Santini's home.

His wife answered. She said she'd put Santini on but not to keep him long. They were getting ready to go out, and their babysitter had just arrived.

Santini came on snapping, "Where've you been all day, Tony? I was trying to get you." And then, not waiting for an answer, he went on, "Did you look at the picture?"

"Yeah."

"And?"

"It might be her," I said hesitantly. "Just *might.*"

"That means it might *not* be her?"

"More likely not," I admitted. "There's something about the picture that's like the blonde I fished out, but—"

"Can't you be more definite?"

"Sorry. Who's the girl in the picture?"

"Name's Sondra Lomax. A B-girl in a joint over on Miami Beach. The Frenzy Club. Ain't that some name for a gyp joint? Her roommate brought the picture in today. Girl named Maria Barreto. Cuban girl. She works in the Frenzy Club, too. Said she hadn't seen or heard from her roommate since Tuesday night."

"The timing fits," I said. "I found her Wednesday morning. Dr. Flanders said she got killed ten to twenty hours before that."

"Sure it fits," Santini said wearily. "You know how many missing blondes I've got that ain't been seen since Tuesday? Nine! No exaggeration. Nine of 'em. And this Sondra Lomax—you know how those B-girls are. They go with the wind. I asked her roommate—Maria Barreto—if she had any reason to think anything violent might've happened to Sondra Lomax. Like did anybody have any reason to kill her? She said no."

"So why did she come to you?" I asked.

"You know how Cubans are. They excite easy. She says the last time she saw Sondra Lomax was at the Frenzy Club Tuesday night. She didn't come home to the apartment they share that night after the club closed. And she still wasn't back Wednesday when Maria woke up. Maria went out, and when she came back Wednesday evening, all Sondra Lomax's clothes and things from their apartment were gone. Except that photo of her that Maria had stuck in one of her own drawers."

"Sounds," I said, "like Maria's roommate just found herself a boyfriend or something and moved out."

"Yeah. But Maria Barreto claims this Lomax girl wouldn't've done that to her. She says they were good friends, that the girl wouldn't skip out without telling her why. Anyway, when she read in the paper about your fishing a blond girl in her twenties out of the ocean, she began to really worry. And when she still hadn't heard from Sondra Lomax today, she decided to come see us, with that picture."

"That's all she had to go on? Didn't she have *any* reason to think her roommate might've ended up in the drink?"

"No," Santini told me through the phone. "No reason at all. She was just worried was all. But I figured there's always a chance. So I took her over to the morgue for a look at your blonde."

"Since when," I asked, "did you turn sadist?"

"Cut it out," he growled angrily. "I had to do it. You know it's routine."

"How'd she take it?"

There was a pause. Santini didn't like telling me. "She took one look at what that shark did and fainted. All we could get out of her was that she couldn't tell."

"How about that little birthmark behind the blonde's ear?" I asked him.

"Maria couldn't remember ever seeing a mark like that."

"Not much of a lead."

"It's less than that," Santini told me. "After this Maria Barreto left, I contacted the guy that runs the Frenzy Club. Danny Yale. He said Sondra Lomax phoned him Wednesday to say she was quitting. She'd met a guy with dough and a yen for her, and she was going to Las Vegas with him."

"If Sondra Lomax made a phone call Wednesday, she certainly isn't the girl I fished out of the water that morning."

"Can't be," Santini agreed.

"Unless," I suggested, "this Danny Yale character lied to you."

"I've got no reason to think so," Santini stated. "Unless you can be more positive about that picture Maria Barreto left with us."

"I can't be," I told him.

"That's that, then," Santini said. "I've got six other leads to missing blondes that're more promising than Sondra Lomax." There was the sound of a woman's angry voice in the background. Santini said quickly, "I've got to sign off now, Tony. My wife's

21

making faces at me. We're gonna look at a new ranch house up in Opa-locka. We need more room, now the kids're getting older."

I said, "Sure. Be seeing you." And hung up.

Before leaving Headquarters, I took another look at the photograph of Sondra Lomax. It still didn't look any more like the face I'd spotted under the water. Not in total. But there *were* features that matched. And there was the cold feeling I got along my spine when I looked too long at the picture.

Considering my own uncertainty, I couldn't blame Santini for not digging further into what had happened to Sondra Lomax. Girls like her breezed in and out of Miami every day without a word to anyone. There was no indication that Sondra Lomax had met with violence—and Santini was a busy man. But me, I wasn't busy. I hadn't worked in three days. I had over a thousand dollars in my pocket, and there was the memory of a dead face that no one but me had seen naggin' in my mind.

I gave the picture back to the desk sergeant and got from him the address of the girl who'd brought it in—Maria Barreto. I went out to my car and drove there.

I figured it was worth half an hour or so to get rid of the nagging doubt. The thought had come to me that Maria Barreto might be able to dig up another photo of her roommate. One in which Sondra Lomax wasn't wearing all that make-up and the phony passion expression. A snapshot, perhaps. If she didn't, I'd forget it.

It was one of those Miami neighborhoods where half the population consists of middle-class Cubans—some refugees from the Batista tyranny, others Batista supporters who'd had to flee Cuba when Castro took over. Back home, their political differences had made these two groups deadly enemies. But in their common exile they managed to live together in fair harmony. On the street where Maria Barreto had shared an apartment with Sondra Lomax, the signs were printed in both English and Spanish. I parked between a mailbox that had LETTERS—CARTAS printed on it and a street sign that said STOP-ALTO. The building itself was a pink-stucco duplex, with a limp and dusty palm tree panting for water in front of it.

The mailbox name plates indicated there were only two apartments. The one belonging to LOMAX—BARRETO occupied the second floor.

The inside door was not locked. It was cool inside. I waited while my eyes adjusted to the dimness. There was a staircase and a short, narrow hall leading past it to the first-floor apartment. I climbed the stairs.

The door at the top had a name tag with LOMAX—BARRETO on it, just like the mailbox in the entry. I knocked and waited. Nothing happened. After a few moments I knocked again. Still no answer.

I glanced at my wrist watch, turned and went back down the steps. I'd try phoning her a little later. If that didn't get her, I could always try the Beach joint where she worked.

I was reaching for the knob of the inside door to the entry when a cold, hard voice spoke behind me.

It said, "Hold it, sonny boy. This is as far as you go."

I turned around slowly, stiffly. I looked at the savage-faced man who'd emerged from under the staircase. And at the shiny Colt .45 automatic in his hand.

4.

"HELLO," I SAID.

Almost anything you say when a guy points a loaded gun at your stomach is likely to sound foolish.

He was big. About six foot four and wide all over. Not fat. Just wide bone and muscle, straining the cheap brown suit he wore. His badly sunburned features looked as though they'd been fashioned with a meat cleaver. Tufts of eyebrows poked out from a heavy ridge of bone. The little finger of his left hand sported a ring with a big diamond. His eyes examined me like surgical knives.

"Let's you 'n' me," he said softly, "go back to that apartment upstairs."

"Nobody's home," I told him.

"I know. I jimmied the lock and had a look a whiles back. Got tired waiting." He gestured impatiently with the automatic. "Upstairs."

I looked into the working end of the .45. I thought about how big a hole a .45 slug would make going into my belly, and the bigger one it would make coming out my back. I climbed back up the steps.

He came behind me. "Don't try kicking back at me or anything," he said to my back. "You can't tell me nothing if you're dead."

I took a deep preparatory breath as I turned the knob at the top of the stairs and stepped inside. Then I tried it. I kicked the door hard with my heel, hoping to slam it shut in his face as I jumped to one side, and snatched the .38 from under my jacket. But he was awfully fast for a man that big. His solid bulk hit the door full force before it could shut. The edge of the door slammed my right shoulder, spinning me off balance and deadening the nerves the length of my arm. He leaped into the room as the .38 jumped out of my hand and hit the rug. I sprang for the gun. He was there before me, down one knee with his big left hand covering my .38. I stopped reaching and froze the way I was, bent over with his eyes and his .45 looking up into my face.

"You got a lot've nerve trying that," he said. "I like a nervy guy. Don't make me blast you before I got a reason to."

I straightened and backed away from him. "We made noise," I pointed out. "The people in the apartment downstairs are probably calling the cops right now."

"Nobody home downstairs," he informed me. He straightened with my .38 in his left hand, glanced around. We were in the living room, which was furnished inexpensively but neatly. One doorway led to a bedroom, another to a big kitchen. He tossed my gun on the sofa across the room, looked me over again. "If you got another gun, I guess it'd be more trouble taking it away from you than taking care of you if you try for it."

"No other gun," I told him,

"Just stand easy, then. No call to get nervous. I only want some info."

"I talk easier without a gun looking at me."

He shook his head. "There's some guys'd like to put holes in me. Maybe you're not one've them, but I can't take the chance. Where's Sondra?"

"I don't know."

"Don't hold out on me, pal," he warned softly. "I'll kick the info out've you if you play it cozy. I been watching this place two days, but Sondra ain't showed. Where's she at?"

"You couldn't have done much of a job of watching," I told him. "She was here some time Wednesday afternoon."

"I *told* you not to con me, bud. I was across the street all yesterday. If she'd showed, I'd've spotted her. There ain't no back door to this place."

I frowned thoughtfully. "Did you see anybody carry any luggage out of here yesterday?"

"A guy. In the afternoon. Came in without anything, went out with two suitcases."

"What did he look like?"

The big bruiser scowled at me. "I'm asking the questions. Where'll I find Sondra? Don't make me ask you again."

"She's supposed to have gone to Las Vegas," I told him. "But I wouldn't vouch for it now."

"Vegas? If that squealing bitch thinks she can get away from me that easy, she's— What'd she do with the boat?"

"What boat?"

He eyed me coldly. "If you're giving me the—What's your connection with Sondra? You her new boyfriend or something?"

"No."

"So what're you doing here? You belong to that hot Spanish broad I seen going in and out of this place?"

"No. I found a dead woman in the ocean Wednesday morning. No one knows who she is. Maria Barreto—she shares this apartment—thought it might be Sondra Lomax. She was worried because she hadn't seen Sondra since Tuesday night."

"Sondra's dead?"

"I don't know. Probably not."

"You said before she went to Vegas."

"That's what somebody said. I'm not so sure. Maybe if you tell me your connection with Sondra Lomax, we can figure out between us where she is."

"It's the boat I want to find first," he growled.

"I don't know what boat you mean. Want to tell me about it? Maybe I can help."

"*Her* boat," he snapped. "I read in the paper about some blonde getting fished out of the water yesterday. What's your name, pal?"

"Anthony Rome."

He nodded slowly. "Yeah. That's the name've the guy that found the blonde. Let's see your wallet."

I got my wallet out. He didn't have to tell me to do it carefully. His gun told me that.

"Toss it."

I threw it to him, underhanded. No tricks. He caught it with his left hand, opened it with his thick fingers and glanced at it. Then he threw it back to me.

As I tucked it back inside my jacket, he said, "The blonde you found in the drink was Sondra?"

"There wasn't enough left of her face for Maria Barreto to tell," I told him. "I came here to see if Maria had a good snapshot of Sondra Lomax. Maybe you do?"

He shook his head. "Why'd anybody else want to kill Sondra?" he asked, puzzled.

"No reason that anybody knows about so far."

"I gotta find that boat," he muttered. He wasn't really telling it to me. He backed to the sofa, keeping an eye on me as he picked up my .38 and ejected the loads. He slipped the bullets into his pocket and dropped the .38 back on the cushion.

"Maybe I'll be talking to that Spanish dish that lives here later," he said. "If I find out you been conning me, I know who you are. I'll come for you."

"I haven't lied to you. If you'll put away the gun and—"

"I gotta go," he snapped. "You try tailing me, you'll wish you hadn't."

A second later he was gone. I heard the heavy pounding of his feet running down the steps. Going to the windows, I poked open one of the Venetian-blind slats, saw him emerge on the pavement below and vanish around the corner. Wiping dampness from my forehead, I walked thoughtfully to the sofa and picked up my empty .38.

5.

THE GIRL SWAYING TO LANGUOROUS MUSIC up on the tiny stage was peeled down to a bra and G-string of black fur. She had pitch-black hair and great dark eyes in a very young face. Her small body was beautifully proportioned. The contrast of black fur and pale flesh achieved its pulse-quickening purpose.

As I entered the place, her slim hands drifted to the fastening of the bra. Pretty, pink-tipped breasts sprang free as she peeled it off and threw it away. The five-piece band broke into a wild cha-cha rhythm. The girl twined her fingers in her jet hair and went wild with it. Small spotlights played over the rippling muscles of her softly curved thighs and belly, her dancing breasts and bare, saucy buttocks. The Frenzy Club was living up to its name.

I'd picked up new loads for my .38 at my office before settling down to a steak-and-eggs dinner in a Biscayne Boulevard grill. I'd taken my time finishing off the meal with a snifter of brandy, while I thought about what the big bruiser had told me. It changed things.

According to Danny Yale, the owner of the Frenzy Club, Sondra Lomax had phoned him Wednesday and said she was heading for Las Vegas with some new boyfriend.

But according to the big man with the .45, it wasn't Sondra who'd gone to the apartment Wednesday afternoon for her clothes. It had been a man.

It was possible that she'd sent her new boyfriend to pick up her things. But it wasn't likely. It would have been much more natural for her to do her own packing—if she could.

I'd thought some more about the face of the blonde in the sea. And the face on that photograph of Sondra Lomax. Then I'd finished my drink and headed across the bay.

Outside, the height of the Miami Beach nightlife was underway. The brilliant, multicolored lighting of Collins Avenue illuminated the white hotels like dream castles and cast a giddy aurora into the dark sky. The old folks in their vacation tans and holiday clothes were already seated in the chairs in front of their hotels on both sides of Collins, absorbed in their favorite after-dinner occupation—watching the healthy young things strut by.

Inside the Frenzy Club, the action had hardly begun. The joints around the Miami area stay open till five in the morning, and business doesn't really perk up till after midnight. But the black-haired girl gyrating up on the tiny stage was doing her best to get the evening off to a hot start.

Standing alone just inside the entrance, I shook my gaze from her writhing nudity and glanced around. The place was done up with chrome, imitation leather, mirrors and black drapes. Only four of the small tables clustered around the stage were occupied. At the long, curved bar, two male customers were hedged in by four girls in daringly cut evening gowns. You can judge the affluence of a Miami Beach strip joint by the looks of its bar girls. These were uniformly young and gorgeous.

I wasn't alone for ten seconds after coming into the Frenzy Club. A tall, willowy redhead with a deep-V neckline exposing the white hills of her thrusting, high-set breasts detached herself from the bar and leeched onto me.

"Looking for a little excitement, dear?" she murmured, flashing an insinuating smile.

"I'm looking for Maria Barreto."

She gave me a look of mock disappointment. "You'll have to wait till she finishes her number." She took my arm and moved close, cushioning the full softness of her bosom against me. "You never can tell what you want till you sample around a little."

I looked at the black-haired stripper on the stage. Maria Barreto.

"You don't want to stick to just one girl," the redhead whispered. "With so much available." She moved her body a little, caressing the tips of her breasts across my arm. "Let's talk it over at the bar."

The Miami Beach B-girls are the best liquor salesmen in the country. They pride themselves on their acquired ability to employ the big tease to strip a mark down to his last dollar.

The bartender was on the spot as we perched side by side on the padded stools. He gave us the knowing grin and asked, "What're you 'n' the lady having?"

I ordered brandies.

A few stools down, a plump little man with a bright sunburn was asking the gilt-haired girl drinking with him, "This place stay open on Sundays?"

"Sure," she told him. "This is a vacation town. Everything's always available if you've got the loot, darling. *Everything.* That's this town's motto. Everything goes."

Miami Beach did have a motto: *Never give a sucker an even break.*

"Doesn't anybody ever sleep in this town?" the plump little man asked.

"Not alone, darling," the girl with the gilt hair said, her voice thick with promise.

That's the other part of the town's motto: *Promise the sucker anything that'll keep him digging into his roll; deliver as little as you can get away with; give him the fast slip when he's busted.*

The bartender brought our drinks. The redhead's brandy was accompanied by the inevitable Coke chaser.

The redhead eyed my roll as I paid the tab. It was fat with my Hialeah winnings. Her thigh pressed against mine. She leaned forward to give me a deeper look into her low-cut bodice and favored me with a dazzling smile. "My name's Annie," she murmured softly. "If you think Maria's something up on that stage, wait'll you see me. I go on next."

"Seen Sondra Lomax around lately?" I asked casually.

"Sondra blew town yesterday. Say, you know a lot of the girls around here, don't you? How come I haven't seen you before?"

"How come she left town?"

"I hear she met some guy with loot, cut out to Las Vegas with him."

"Who's the guy?"

Annie shrugged. "Dunno." She picked up her brandy and poured it in her mouth. I watched her throat. She didn't swallow. She picked up her Coke chaser and made like she was drinking from it. But the level of the Coke didn't go down; it went up. She'd emptied her mouthful of brandy into the Coke. Which is why B-girls are known in the trade as spit-backs. The girls aren't supposed to get drunk. Just the suckers.

"I guess Sondra played around with lots of guys," I suggested.

"Sondra? Not her. She was always too gone on Larry Score. And him two-timing her with half the broads in town. I guess she finally got smart."

"Who's Larry Score?"

The redhead sighed and made a kissing motion with her red lips. "A living doll. Cary Grant ain't got a thing on Larry."

On the tiny stage, Maria Barreto stomped her dance to a halt and stood there quivering, feet planted, far apart, arms outflung. She was breathing hard and her body gleamed wetly in the spotlights. As she vanished through the side curtains to a spatter of applause, the redhead beside me said, "I got to get ready to go on now. Buy me another quickie to get me in the mood?"

"After you get back, maybe."

She grinned at me and showed the tip of her pink tongue between her sharp white teeth. "Oh, you're a smart one. Want to see more of the merchandise first, that it?" She patted my cheek. "Well, you watch good, lover. I'll be dancing just for you." She slid off the stool and swivel-hipped her way through a door beside the stage.

A skinny m.c. had taken over the stage, spewing a steady stream of double-meaning remarks about Maria Barreto's performance. I nursed my drink and waited. Two tables had been pushed together against the stage to accommodate a party of six youngsters—three girls and three boys. The m.c. began prodding them with questions, learned they were three recently married couples.

He fixed them with a look that should have warned them.

"Just *how* long you kids been doin' it legal?"

"Two days," one of the boys mumbled nervously.

The little m.c. leered. "And you're all down here on your honeymoon together?"

They were.

"What an *orgy!*" The m.c. heaved a big sigh and gazed. heavenward—or at the ceiling of the Frenzy Club, which was close as he'd ever get. He launched into a series of filthy honeymoon jokes.

The three fresh young couples at the table responded to each joke with forced laughs. All except one husky young bride. She fixed her groom with a stony stare, her mouth thin and tight as the color rose in her face. Her brand-new husband, more embarrassed by this than by the m.c.'s jokes, looked away from her and continued to force his laughter, playing hard at being a good sport. His young bride sat with her body rigid and her face frozen, like a statue commemorating an ancient anger.

Maria Barreto emerged from the door beside the stage and came along the bar. Wearing a black sheath gown scooped low in front and with her raven hair piled atop her pretty head, she looked even younger than she had on the stage. And strangely innocent. She spotted me and came straight toward me. The redhead had obviously tipped her off.

"Hi," she said, pretending she remembered me. "I was hoping you'd come back." She assumed I was some guy who'd been in before and liked her. The girls seldom remembered any of the constant stream of suckers.

"My name's Anthony Rome," I told her. It didn't register at first. Her mind was on performing her job.

"That's a very nice name," she said, with just a touch of Spanish accent. She slid up onto the stool beside me as the bartender appeared. "Buy me a drink? I'm always very thirsty after I dance."

"I'm the one who found the blonde in the ocean," I told her.

She lost her professional smile abruptly. "Oh—I—" She saw the bartender gazing at us fixedly, glanced at me apologetically.

I nodded. The bartender went for her drink.

"Did you look at the picture of Sondra?" Maria Barreto asked me quickly.

"Yes. But I couldn't be sure. Have you got any snapshots?"

Maria shook her head. "That was the only picture of her I had. I'm afraid I bothered the police for nothing. It turns out Sondra is all right She just went away."

The bartender brought Maria's apricot brandy and Coke chaser. She ignored it. He looked pointedly at my unfinished drink. I ignored him.

"When'd you find that out?" I asked Maria.

"Tonight."

"Who told you?"

"Mr. Yale. He owns this place. He was very angry with me for going to the police about Sondra."

"Why?"

"He said he doesn't like the cops poking around him. He said I was stupid. I guess he's right. Sondra called him yesterday, told him she was going away with some man. So she's all right."

"Who's the man?"

Maria shrugged. "I don't know. She didn't tell Mr. Yale his name."

"I thought Sondra had a steady boyfriend. Larry Score."

She nodded. "Larry was never steady with her. She was steady with him. She's been crazy about him for years."

"How about you?" I asked her. "Have you got a steady boyfriend, too?"

Her dark eyes clouded. "I have a husband."

That was one reason the suckers who hoped to get these girls drunk enough to stagger out with them didn't have a chance. They all either were married or had boyfriends.

"You and your husband separated?" I asked.

"My husband," she said somberly, "is in prison in Havana. I would be, too. But I got away."

I didn't probe further along that line. It was an old story.

There was hardly a Cuban refugee in Florida who didn't have someone in prison back home. No matter which side of the political war in Cuba they played, it sooner or later turned out to be the wrong side.

"So you no longer believe it was Sondra Lomax I found?"

"I guess not. It can't be."

"But you did think it might be, before. Why?"

"She went away without saying anything to me," Maria explained. "We were good friends. She even left me stuck with all the rent to pay. I never thought she would do such a thing to me."

"Was Sondra from Cuba, too?" I asked her.

"Oh, no. She is a native of Florida. From Jacksonville."

"I was to your place earlier this evening," I told her. "But you weren't in."

"I didn't go back," she said. "After the police made me look at—" Her face got sick-looking, remembering the corpse in the morgue. "I was very upset. I went to a double-feature movie, then just walked around till it was time to come here to work."

"There was a man at your apartment," I told her. "Looking for Sondra." I described him carefully.

Maria Barreto shook her head. "I don't know who he is."

I dropped that. "Who's this Larry Score?"

"He does some kind of work for a man named Al Mungo."

That silenced me for a few moments. I knew about Al Mungo.

He'd once been the most powerful mobster in the West Coast branch of the syndicate. But four years in a federal prison on an income-tax-evasion rap had ended his active career. After getting out, the aging Mungo had retired to a Miami mansion on Biscayne Bay. But the word was that he still kept his hand in, and could be a bad one to mess with.

I focused on Maria Barreto again. "Do you know anything about any boat belonging to Sondra?"

"She *had* a boat. Lost it two months ago. I was there when it happened. I almost got drowned."

"It sank?"

"Yes. Sondra took me and some of the other girls for a ride in the boat. We hit a rock, near Elliot Key. The boat sank. It was a good thing we could all swim. We swam to Elliot Key and a nice man with a yacht picked us all up and brought us back to Miami. It was a shame. It was a very nice boat. With a little cabin and all. Her boyfriend gave it to her."

"Larry Score?"

"Him? He never gave Sondra anything. Another boyfriend, Earl Gronsky. He's from Jacksonville, like Sondra. She said he was always after her. So one time when she got mad at Larry for giving her the runaround, she decided to hell with Larry, and made the scene for a while with Earl Gronsky."

"What's this Earl Gronsky look like?" I asked her.

"I don't know," Maria said. "I only know Sondra six months, since I came to work here. Gronsky went to prison a couple years ago. I guess he's still there."

"What'd he go up for?"

"Holding up a gas station. Sondra said he was very tough, everybody was afraid of him. Even Larry Score. Only Sondra wasn't afraid of him."

"Lieutenant Santini told me the last time you saw Sondra was Tuesday night," I remarked.

"Yes. In here. About midnight. Larry Score and Mr. Yale were drinking with Gretchen Forrest. They were going to have a party or something at her house. They took Sondra along with them."

She didn't have to explain who Gretchen Forrest was. Gretchen Forrest's name and picture were always popping up in the society pages and gossip columns—and sometimes on the front pages. Her story was public property. A nerve-wracked, much-married heiress who followed the international set's annual migration from one luxury resort to another, she was currently sojourning in her Miami home. She had as many problems as she had dollars, apparently. Liquor—and the wrong kind of men—were always getting her into trouble. According to what I'd read, psychiatry had failed her, along with yoga, religion and dabbling in the arts. She just kept getting into trouble. And kept buying her way out.

I frowned at Maria Barreto. "Sondra never came back to your apartment from this party?"

Maria shrugged, looking uncertain. "She must have. She came and took out all her things yesterday afternoon, when I wasn't there."

I asked, "Exactly what does Yale say she—"

I stopped in mid-sentence. A hard hand had closed on my shoulder, was turning me around.

I turned and looked at a short, stocky, hard-faced man in a white dinner jacket. His dark hair was slicked straight back on his round skull. His eyes were small, pale and mean.

His hand dropped from my shoulder. "I'm Danny Yale," he said quietly. "Why're you asking questions about me?"

Maria said quickly, "Mr. Yale, this is the man who found that girl in the ocean yesterday."

A nerve jumped in his cheek. But otherwise the expression of his face didn't change. "So? Why come nosing around here? I already told the cops Maria was just being stupid. It couldn't've been Sondra. You brought up that blond broad yesterday morning. I heard from Sondra yesterday afternoon. So that's it."

"You didn't see Sondra Lomax yesterday, did you?" I asked him.

"No. She phoned me. I told the cops that."

"Are you sure it was Sondra Lomax who phoned you?"

"Sure I'm sure. She worked for me over a year. I know her voice."

"Must have been a pretty sudden decision on her part to leave town," I said. "Just the night before she left, she went out to a party with you. She say anything to you about it then?"

He eyed me unpleasantly. His lips thinned. He said through his teeth, "I read in the paper you're a private eye."

"That's right."

"I guess that explains it," he said softly. "You're trying to drum up a little business for yourself. Maybe blackmail business?"

"You're making me mighty curious," I told him. "What objections have you got to answering a few questions?"

"I already answered them," he said flatly. "To the cops. The *real* cops. Which you ain't. So get out of here. Before I throw you out."

"You can try, if you need the exercise," I told <u>him</u>, not moving.

He hesitated, glanced at the bartender. I glanced that way, too. The bartender had one hand under the bar, out of sight.

Danny Yale looked back to me. "This is my place. You get out, or I call the cops and tell 'em you're trying to make trouble. I got connections. And you got a private-eye license that's real easy to lose."

There was no percentage in staying. Yale wasn't going to tell me anything. Neither was Maria Barreto—with Yale there. I turned to her. "I'll be seeing you again. After you finish work here."

As I got off the stool, the skinny little m.c. had abandoned the tiny stage to Annie, the redhead. The band started a turgid, thump-punctuated number as she slithered out through the curtains wearing a leopard costume. Her pelvis jerked to the thud of the drum, sending out a message in universal code. I. walked out of the Frenzy Club with Danny Yale's mean little eyes boring holes in my back.

My Oldsmobile was parked in a side street off Collins, four

blocks away. I slid behind the wheel, lit a Lucky and sat there thinking it over. Finally, I decided to go have a talk with the notorious Gretchen Forrest

I've made decisions that turned out worse.

But not many.

6.

IT WAS ONE OF THOSE EXCLUSIVE, artificially constructed residential islands in Biscayne Bay. There was a short bridge leading to it off the causeway spanning the bay between Miami Beach and Miami. I turned the Olds off the causeway onto the bridge, entered the dark, palm-and-pine-hedged driveway circling the island. Few lights showed. High stone walls and dense fragrant-flowered shrubbery cloaked the island's houses from the drive. But I'd seen them before, passing by with my boat. Big homes cuddled in the embrace of lush green foliage dotted with flowers of every hue. Mediterranean-style villas of pink-and-white concrete-block stucco with red tile roofs. Each with its giant-size pool and private boat dock.

There was no sound but the swish of my tires and the whispering of the breeze stirring the tops of the high palms outlined against the star-filled sky. I drove slowly, my headlights tunneling through the darkness till they caught a small sign that said FORREST. I parked by the entrance to the private drive and went in under a series of Grecian arches with vines clinging to their stone pillars. The low, tile-roofed Mediterranean villa had an antique door of wrought iron. There was no doorbell in sight. I raised the heavy iron clapper attached to the door and banged it.

The door was opened by a stately, white-haired Negro manservant in black trousers and a white jacket

"Yes, sir?" he inquired softly.

"Gretchen Forrest in?"

"Whom shall I say is calling, sir?"

"Mr. Rome."

He motioned politely for me to step inside. He murmured, "If you will wait here for a moment, sir."

After he vanished, I looked around the vast, marble-floored living room. To my untrained eye, its furniture looked merely old, too ornate and rather fragile. But I guessed it represented a small fortune shoveled out to European antique dealers. A big crystal chandelier dripped from the center of the high ceiling, reflecting in the wall mirrors. Across the marble floor, the living room proper was marked off by floor-to-ceiling ivory pillars. Beyond those, the room opened into a lush courtyard surrounding a tile-bordered swimming pool.

Beyond the pool, where the tall, thin mast of a catboat swung, a girl was striding off the dock toward me. She wore sandals, white shorts and blouse, and she moved with a kind of lanky grace that advertised a lot of restless energy. When she entered the light, I saw her roan-colored hair and the delicate loveliness of her fine-boned face. Her neatly curved figure was slender, the top of her head about shoulder height to me. She looked strangely familiar.

This wasn't Gretchen Forrest. She was too young—in fact and in spirit. As she came through the ivory pillars into the room, she hesitated, looking at me curiously. There was nothing shy about her appraisal. A hard core of independent self-assurance showed in her stance.

She said, "Hi, there," and crossed the marble floor toward me, "Looking for someone?"

"Miss Forrest."

"Which one? There's two of us, you know. I'm Kit."

"Your sister."

She said, "Oh." Close up, I saw the spray of freckles across the bridge of her cute nose, masked by her golden tan. Her mouth was bold and stubborn. Her large eyes, green in depth like the sea over a coral reef, studied me gravely. "I have the feeling I know you from somewhere. Do I?"

I'd remembered by then. "You've been playing the horses a lot this season."

She laughed. She had a nice laugh, too. "You've been looking at my deflated bank balance."

"I've seen you at the track. And once across the roulette wheel at Reggie's." Reggie's was an illegal but well-protected gambling casino outside Miami.

"Well, well," Kit Forrest murmured. "Hello, fellow gambler. And how've the ponies been treating *you?*"

"I was on Silly Boy in the last race this afternoon."

"You bet Silly Boy! How did you know? A tip?"

"A hunch."

She grimaced in mock outrage. "All my hunches ever get me is a handful of tickets to tear up. I'll have to let you take me to the track someday so I can ride your luck. Who are you?"

"My name's Rome. Anthony Rome."

"Do you do something?"

"Now and then."

"Like what?"

"I'm a private detective."

"Oh? That's interesting. Are you supposed to be detecting something around here?"

"Know a girl named Sondra Lomax?" I asked her.

She shook her head. "It doesn't ring a bell. Who is she?"

"She worked at a place called the Frenzy Club."

Kit Forrest wrinkled her nose as though she smelled something. "That'd be part of Gretchen's crowd. I keep my own bad company." She eyed me gravely again. "Odd I didn't notice you at the track or Reggie's. You remembered me."

"You're more noticeable." I grinned to take the edge off the flattery.

She grinned back and then glanced at her wrist watch.

"Give me a call sometime, Tony. We'll hit the ponies together. Pool hunches. Right now I've got to run. I'm late for a beach party."

I opened the door for her, watched her run to the long, three-car garage siding the house. She ran like a colt, with the same young awkwardness and inbred grace. A few seconds later, the muted roar of a sports-car engine came from the garage. Kit Forrest whipped out in an open white Mark IX Jaguar, flashed the length of the drive with the headlights stabbing the darkness and was gone.

As I closed the door and turned back, Gretchen Forrest came through a draped archway to my right.

She wore green toreador pants and a black Russian blouse that clung to the curves of her full-blown figure. She'd been a damned attractive girl. When she'd been a girl. Too much drink and too little sleep and too many emotional explosions had taken their toll.

Her features were a lot like those of her kid sister. But the difference between them hit you stronger than the resemblance. It was more than age. Kit Forrest was in her early twenties; Gretchen only somewhere in her early thirties. Her boldly curved figure was still a good one, and the gold dye job on her short-cropped hair wasn't unbecoming. But life, somewhere along the line, had kicked the props out from under Gretchen Forrest's ego; and whatever she held it up with now wasn't doing an adequate job. She showed all the edgy signs of going on frayed nerves alone.

"Was that Kit who just drove off?" she asked, her voice a bit slurred.

I told her it was.

"Damn that girl," she said irritably. "Can't stay still in one place for two seconds. I wanted to tell her—"

She caught control of herself abruptly, looked me over nervously, almost anxiously. "Sam said your name is Rome. Am I supposed to know you?"

"I'm a private detective, Miss Forrest," I told her. "I also happen to have found a murdered woman in the ocean Wednesday

42

morning. Maybe you read about it in the papers."

Her face came apart. She put it back together again, but not quite like it had been before.

"I never read the papers any more," she said thickly. "I prefer the horror movies on TV."

"You threw a party here late Tuesday night," I said. "Guess it went on quite a while?"

"Excuse me," she murmured distractedly, "what was it you wanted to know?" And then, not giving me a chance to answer, "Where are my manners? I know, don't tell me. They're always lousy, but—There's no need to stand here like two bumps. Let's sit down."

She led the way across the room to a long, ancient couch backing two of the ivory pillars. "Here. Make yourself comfortable."

I sat down cautiously. Not sure if the couch would hold me. The exterior might have been antique, but its insides were strictly up-to-date springs and foam rubber. Gretchen Forrest perched herself on the edge of a fragile-looking wing chair.

Before I could say anything, she popped up again. "Let me make us some drinks, first," she blurted.

"I've had a drink. About that party you—"

"I've had a drink, too," she said. "But I always seem to need another." She went to a short, tapestry-covered bar on one side of the room, began mixing herself a Martini. "This bar—it was originally something in a Spanish monastery. Isn't it ghastly? Father had such stinking taste."

I waited, wondering if she'd just run down if I let her alone.

She came back to her wing chair, perched in it again and took a gulp of her Martini. "Do you know about Father? I guess you do. Everybody does. He was—"

"Sondra Lomax was here at your party Tuesday night, wasn't she?" I demanded, cutting her short.

"Oh. Sondra." She finished off her Martini thirstily. "Yes. She was here. *Everybody* was here, eventually."

"What time did she leave here that night?"

Gretchen Forrest shrugged her shoulders. "I didn't notice. It was one of those parties that just grew and grew, you know the kind. So many people, half of them I didn't even know, coming in and going out all the time. And to tell you the truth, I got pretty damn plastered while the shindig was still young."

"You didn't notice who she left with?"

She avoided my eyes. "No. I told you. There were so many people here that—"

"All right, Miss Forrest," a heavy voice said behind me, "*we'll* take care of him now."

Not turning around, I let my hand drift up my leg toward the gun in my belt holster.

"Don't," another, thinner voice said to my left. "We'll blow your brains out, you try it."

I stopped my hand where it was on my thigh. Gretchen Forrest had dropped her Martini glass to the carpet and was on her feet, swaying, her face ashen.

"Link your fingers behind your head, Rome," the heavier voice behind me said. "Then stand up easy."

I got my hands together at the back of my neck and stood up.

"Please," Gretchen Forrest rasped, "don't—do anything to him. Just—"

"Just leave it to us," the heavy voice told her respectfully.

She gave me one last, misery-blurred look, then fled.

"Turn around, Rome."

I turned. Both of the men standing between the pillars behind the couch had guns. Identical Smith & Wesson Magnums. One of the men had the massive bulk of a pro-football player gone just a little bit soft, and the face of a good-natured ape. The other was shorter, trimmer, except for the wide shoulders. His brutal face was dotted with maybe a million red freckles.

"Where d'you wear your gun?" the massive, ape-faced one demanded. Oddly, he was the one with the thinner voice.

You don't play guessing games with two heavy Magnums

looking you in the face. "My belt," I said.

Ape-face did a cautious, professional job of taking my .38 and frisking me for any other hidden weapons. Then he moved off a bit to my left, so the two of them were flanking me.

"Okay," he told Freckles. "He's clean now."

"Let's go," Freckles told me, gesturing toward the courtyard outside the house.

"My car's out front," I said, thinking of the little gun taped under my dashboard. "You're not playing it smart, leaving it here."

"We'll take care of the car. After you get taken care of. Right now we take a little walk. Move!"

I started through the pillars, nerves twitching in my legs. I resisted the suicidal urge to run.

"Exactly what's supposed to happen to me?" I asked tightly as they walked me down to the dark waters of the bay.

I was told, "That's up to Al Mungo."

7.

I FIGURED IT AS THEY MARCHED ME ALONG the dark, empty beach. The only time Gretchen could have phoned for the marines was right after her manservant had announced me to her. So my name alone had been enough to alarm her. I thought back to Danny Yale at the Frenzy Club. Gretchen Forrest had been warned I might be around, asking questions she wouldn't want to answer. I wondered how the Marines had managed to arrive so fast.

I found out the place they walked me to was just around the other side of the island.

From the rear, the villa looked like a twin to the Forrest place. We went up to a grove of palms surrounding a marble-tiled terrace illuminated by pink floodlights. In the middle of the terrace was an enormous curved swimming pool, its water lighted from underneath. A man in white slacks and a violet-flowered sports shirt lounged in a bamboo chair by the poolside, watching a girl swim.

As we came onto the terrace, the man turned his head and looked at us. Al Mungo. Anyone who'd ever seen his picture in the papers would have recognized <u>him</u>. Age had taken most of the hair from his skull, but it hadn't altered <u>him</u> much in any other way. He still looked like he could cut your heart out and eat it before breakfast.

His eyes jumped to the two hoods standing just out of reach on either side of me.

"He clean?" His voice had the incisive bite of a whiplash.

"Sure, boss," Ape-face told him.

"So why're you waving the artillery around? This ain't—isn't no wild West show."

The two hoods hurriedly put their Magnums out of sight. But their hands stayed in their pockets with the guns.

"That's better," I said. "They were making me nervous."

"*Stay* nervous," Al Mungo advised bluntly. "They can do more damage without the iron. Shev."—he jerked a thumb at the freckled hood with the heavyweight shoulders on the welterweight body—" Shev used to be pretty good in the ring. Frenchy played pro football with the Los Angeles Rams."

So I'd guessed right about Ape-face.

Al Mungo turned his head and yelled at the girl in the water. "Audrey!"

She swam over, got her hands on the tile side of the pool and looked up at us blank-faced. She was a pretty girl with a soft face and very white skin that hadn't been touched by our Florida sun. Strictly a nighttime doll.

"Company," she said in a little-girl voice, looking at me. "That's nice." She didn't sound like she really cared.

"Not company for you," Mungo told her. "Go lose yourself for a while."

Docilely, the girl grasped the iron pool ladder and climbed out, dripping water on the terrace. The red bikini she wore wouldn't have furnished enough material to diaper a newborn baby. The pale white body straining those two bits of red cloth was phenomenal.

"Okay if I go for a drive in the new Caddy?" she asked Mungo.

"So long as you bring it back in one piece."

She glanced at me, murmured, "Nice to've met you." The way she walked off into the house revealed how aware she was of the devastating effect of her body in motion.

When she was gone, Mungo got down to business abruptly.

"You were bothering Miss Forrest." He said it as though he were accusing me of spitting on the flag.

I didn't say anything. I was figuring my chance of grabbing his throat before a bullet got me and using him as my ticket out of there. The odds were murderous.

"Gretchen Forrest," Al Mungo informed me, "is real class. Top society. Maybe you didn't know that."

"She *must* be class. That's all there is on this island. Including the classiest gangsters."

Mungo stared at me for two heavy heartbeats. "I'm out of the rackets. No different from any retired legit businessman. Respectable. And Gretchen Forrest happens to be a friend of mine."

"That proves she's class, all right," I said.

Mungo's gash of a mouth twisted. Frenchy's huge left hand slapped my ear with the force and weight of a wet sandbag. I stumbled sideways with my brain ringing, the whole side of my head going numb where he'd hit me.

As I caught my balance, fighting the rage bubbling up inside of me, a new voice snapped irritably, "What *is* this?"

The voice belonged to a tall boy who'd appeared from among the palms surrounding the terrace. He was in his mid-twenties, and he wore leather-thong sandals, skintight dungarees and a soiled white polo shirt. He was a younger, softer version of Al Mungo. The softness was in his face, not in his long, bony frame. A spoiled, defensive expression had taken up permanent residence with him. It went with his go-to-hell slouch.

"Go away, Paul," Al Mungo told him gently. "This isn't any of your business."

"Nothing you do is," Paul Mungo responded peevishly.

"Thank God. And don't worry, I'm going. I'll be out late tonight."

"Got another date with Kit?" Al Mungo asked him with a paternal grin that didn't become him.

"That," Paul Mungo snapped, "is none of *your* business."

"If you're going out with Kit, you ought to dress nice. It ain't right she should always see you lookin' like a slob."

Paul Mungo turned on his heel and slouched away through the house.

"Such a boy," Mungo murmured fondly, watching him go. "My beatnik son."

He turned back to me. "You know what? I think Paul and Kit—that's Gretchen Forrest's kid sister—are gonna end up getting married one've these days. What d'you think've that?"

I was disappointed in Kit Forrest. I didn't say it.

On the other side of the house, a car started up and roared away. A few seconds later, another car did the same.

"That," Mungo went on, "will make me related to Gretchen Forrest. Al Mungo related to the Forrest family. The cream've society. Ain't that something for a guy like me, that started out without a dime to my name?"

"It's something, all right," I agreed.

"So you see why I ain't gonna let a cheap creep like you annoy Miss Forrest."

"A girl named Sondra Lomax was at a party in the Forrest house Tuesday night," I said. "All I want to know is when she left, and with whom. Maybe *you* can tell me?"

"I wouldn't know anything about it."

"Maybe Larry Score would. I understand he and the Lomax girl were pretty close. Score around?"

"You don't listen good, do you," Mungo whispered. "I just warned you about something."

"I got another warning last night. By phone. Maybe that one was from you, too?"

"How," Mungo wondered aloud, "did a guy as dumb as you manage to live this long?" He glanced at Frenchy and Shev, nodded.

The two hoods brought their hands out of their pockets. Without the guns.

I kicked Frenchy in the shin.

He yelled and jerked up his hurt leg, balancing on his other foot I balled my fists and swung the right one, getting all the driving

49

power of my shoulders and back behind it. My knuckles bent painfully as they slammed off the side of Frenchy's jaw. He floundered backward. Half the water in the pool mushroomed upward as he went in.

I spun around. Shev's fist whizzed past my face. I slipped inside the punch, put my forehead on his right shoulder and hit him twice in the stomach, as low and as hard as I could. His abdominal muscles were like bands of iron. But he felt it. It bent him. His eyes went wide, hurt and surprised. He twisted out of reach before I could do more damage.

The next second he was coming in at me again in a boxer's crouch, left fist stabbing out, right cocked back. Al Mungo was on his feet, watching.

Shev jabbed the left at my eyes. I ducked—into a right that came at me like a bullet. It struck me squarely between the eyes. Pain exploded behind my forehead. My vision blurred: I flew backward and hit the terrace with the backs of my shoulders. Instinctively, I rolled as I landed to avoid a kick, scrambled on my hands and knees and lurched up to my feet with my vision clearing. Shev was feinting the left at my face again. This time I didn't flinch from it. Instead, I caught his left wrist with both hands and tugged, the pull joining the forward movement of his jab to yank him off balance. I twisted his wrist, got my thumbs against the back of his hand and applied sharp pressure. Shev hit the terrace tiles on his ear. I kicked him in the face, felt the satisfying crunch as his nose caved in.

Then Frenchy's big, dripping-wet arms were wrapping around my neck, pulling me back against his chest, lifting me off my feet.

Shev got up with tears and blood dripping down his snarling face. He launched himself at me, slamming a fist into my stomach. Nausea and agony spasmed my insides. I jerked up my legs, took his next stomach slam on my knee. My legs snapped straight out. The heels of my shoes thudded against Shev's chest, bowled him backward off his feet.

Frenchy's wet arms tightened across my throat, cutting off my air. I jerked my right hand back over my shoulder. My thumb found one of his eyes. He screamed and let go of me.

I hit the tiles on my knees. Shev was already bouncing back up on his feet, coming at me. I got one foot under me and dove at him head first, butting him in the stomach and knocking him down again. Straightening, I started to turn. Not fast enough. One of Frenchy's ham-like fists caught the back of my neck. I stumbled forward fighting for balance. My ankles tangled, and I was back down on my hands and knees. There was no time to roll or try getting up. I braced my weight on my hands and kicked both feet backward like a mule.

My heels cracked against Frenchy's ankles and shot them out from under him. He crashed down beside me. I came up on my knees and slashed the hard edge of my stiff-held hand at the back of his neck. Frenchy twisted just in time to take it on the side of his hard skull. Pain shot up my arm to the shoulder. But Frenchy's head bounced off the tiles.

I was pulling back my hand for another slice at his neck when Al Mungo stepped in and kicked me neatly in the temple.

I flopped over with darkness swirling all around me—all out of fight but not quite unconscious. My efforts to get up were ineffectual. The terrace heaved and rolled under me like a boat in a squall.

From somewhere far off, Mungo's voice said: *"Now* can you two pansies handle <u>him</u>?"

I felt myself gripped by the armpits, dragged upright through the swirling blackness.

Mungo spoke again: "Rome, this time I just tell you and make sure you get that I mean it. Drum up business someplace else. If there's a next time, I'll soak your clothes with alcohol and put a match to you."

Something hard drilled through the black fog and got me in the stomach. My tongue seemed to get too big for my mouth.

Another something slammed the point of my chin; then the side of my head; then—I whirlpooled downward and left whatever else it was that they did to me far behind.

The bottom of that whirlpool was a snug, secure, safe place to stay. I fought against coming up out of it. Sick pain was waiting on the surface. I opened my eyes. A little. I lay folded on my side on the front seat of my Olds.

My clothes smelled strongly of whisky. They'd splashed a lot of it over the front of me. My cut and swollen mouth burned from the liquor they'd poured between my teeth.

The darkness inside my head ebbed but the darkness outside remained. It was still night. My first attempt at straightening ripped a high-pitched moan out of me. My middle felt like they'd torn out my stomach and replaced it with a sack full of hot broken glass.

I pressed both hands against the hurt and lay still, experiencing a dreamlike ebb and flow of consciousness. My wrist was pressed against something hard. My .38. They'd stuck it back in my holster, probably still fully loaded. My key was probably in the ignition, too. There was no way of proving I hadn't just got clobbered in a drunken alley brawl.

After a time I tried straightening a bit again. It was easier this time. So I got an elbow under me and sat up. A mistake. Hard, deadening fingers squeezed my brain. I just had time to cradle my forearms and head on the steering wheel before I passed out cold again.

I had no way of knowing how long I was gone that time. When I opened my eyes again and cautiously lifted my head from the steering wheel, the first streaks of dawn were graying the sky.

With my elbows braced on the wheel, I squinted through the windshield. My Olds was parked at the curb of a residential street somewhere in Miami. I didn't know exactly where. And I couldn't seem to care much.

I was just sitting there, waiting futilely for time to heal me, when I suddenly remembered that I was late for an appointment. For some reason it felt terribly important that I keep that date as soon as possible.

Maybe I blanked out again. Maybe I just sat there staring at nothing. But the next <u>thing</u> I saw was this lighted cab cruising down the street in my direction.

I opened my mouth to yell through the open window. All that came out was a croaking sound. I got both hands on the horn and pressed. The horn blasted the stillness of the street to shreds. I kept leaning on it till the cab drew to a halt beside my car.

"What's the matter, Jack?" the cab driver called. "Stalled or something?"

I nodded my head. I was careful about it, but a couple firecrackers went off between my ears anyway.

"There's a gas station open all night over on Seventeenth," he said. "I can take you there, if you want."

I got hold of the door handle, opened it and shoved myself out of the Olds. My legs had no more starch in them than rubber bands. They folded as soon as I got both feet on the street. I went down on my knees and stayed that way, my head sagging. I didn't try to get up. I was having enough to do just staying up on my knees.

The cab driver said, "Oh! Drunk, huh? Boy, this's my night for 'em." He got out of his cab and squatted down beside me, his bright eyes looking at my face. "You want I should take you some place, Jack?"

I nodded. He straightened, opened the rear door of his cab. "It'll cost you an extra fiver, Jack. I'm always takin' a chance you'll toss your cookies inside my hack."

I made the effort, finally managed to rasp, "Okay."

He helped me up off the street. Between us, we got me onto the cab's rear seat. I slumped back, my head against the cushion.

He looked in at me. "Know where you want to go? Or should I see in your wallet where you belong?"

I took my time about it and managed to clear my throat and think hard at the same time, I rasped out Maria Barreto's address.

It wasn't sensible, and I knew it and didn't care. There was only one place I should have been heading—to bed; or maybe to a doctor. But a blind, crazy stubbornness was <u>impelling</u> me now. The way I felt kept me reminded of what I owed Mungo and his thugs.

It was a debt I was going to pay back—in spades.

That was part of what drove me. The other part was that they'd done it to stop me from digging any deeper into the matter of Sondra Lomax. So now nothing was going to stop me.

I wasn't aware of going back to sleep until the cab driver's hand shaking my shoulder brought me awake.

"Okay, Jack. This is where you said."

I blinked to clear my eyes, peered at the two-story stucco apartment building.

"Can you do it?" the cab driver asked.

"Let's see," I croaked.

My knees held this time. I fished the wad of bills out of my pocket. It all seemed to be there still. With fumbling fingers, I peeled a five and two ones into the cabbie's hand. With him watching anxiously, I trudged stiff-legged across the pavement into the building.

Inside, I got through the entry, to the bottom of the inner stairs. Hanging onto the rail, I started up, concentrating on making it one step at a time.

The door with LOMAX-BARRETO on it was open. I trudged inside.

I didn't feel much surprise. But my legs began to go rubbery on me again, and I knew if I didn't sit down I was going to fall down.

So I sat down. On the floor. Beside Maria Barreto.

The bulging eyes in her gorged face stared up at me like dark-colored marbles.

A police-car siren wailed somewhere in the distance.

8.

THE FIRST TIME LIEUTENANT SANTINI WOKE ME UP it was about
noon. I was sound asleep in my cell in the Dade County
Courthouse, where I'd been since the police doctor pronounced me
bruised, battered and suffering from a badly shocked nervous
system—but otherwise sound.

"You must have the constitution of an ox," the doctor had said.
"Considering the beating you took, it's a minor miracle you've got
no broken bones, internal hemorrhage or brain concussion."

"It wasn't from lack of trying," I'd told him.

As soon as my cell door clanged open, I came awake with my
mind functioning coherently for the first time since the sharp point
of Al Mungo's shoe had connected with my temple. I sat up on my
slab feeling like one enormous bruise—but with no resulting
dizziness.

"Okay," Santini greeted me, "you're out."

"The cab driver backed up my story, I take it."

"You got a better break than that, Tony." He told me about it.

Shortly before I'd arrived at Maria Barreto's apartment, the
elderly couple living in the apartment below had been wakened by
the pounding steps of someone running down the inner stairs.
Through their front windows, they'd seen a man charge out of the

building and run away up the street.

"A big man," Santini told me. "Wearing a brown suit that looked too tight for him. That's all the description they could give us."

The woman in the downstairs apartment had decided to go up and see if anything was wrong. She found the door open, saw Maria Barreto on the floor, strangled to death, and phoned for the cops. She and her husband had seen me arrive shortly before the police.

"So I'm off the hook," I said. "And you figure this big man in the brown suit is the one who strangled Maria Barreto."

Santini nodded. "Not much of a description. If he changes that suit, we've got nothing. We can't pick up every big man in the county."

I had a hunch I could tell him who his man was. But I didn't. I wanted to get to him before the cops got him. He was the sort who'd instinctively clam up if a cop asked him anything—even the time of day.

Leaving the cell with Santini, I decided to hang around while he checked out the rest of my story—my assault-and-battery charge. After Santini headed out, I sat in his office for a time, smoking. But the hurt and the weariness began to grip me again. So I took one of the pills the doctor had given me, went down the hall to the Headquarters locker room and stretched out on one of the bunks.

The next time Santini woke me it was four in the afternoon.

He'd brought a bag full of lunch from a diner. We sat on the bunk and had a sandwich each, washing the food down with coffee from cardboard containers.

"You've got no case against anybody," Santini told me as we ate.

"I figured," I said. "I was just wondering what kind of story they'd rigged to get out from under."

Santini chewed down a mouthful of bread and ham, swallowed some of the coffee. "Gretchen Forrest says you came to her place to ask about Sondra Lomax. You wanted to know when the Lomax girl left Tuesday night, and with whom. Miss Forrest says she doesn't know. There were too many people, and she'd had a lot to drink. She says she told you that, and you left."

"Did she say how I left?"

"You just said goodbye and walked out."

"Gretchen Forrest is a very shaky dame," I said. "You could have squeezed more of the truth than that out of her."

"Squeeze? Gretchen Forrest? You got any idea just who she is?"

"Yeah," I said disgustedly. "She's about thirty million dollars' worth of influence."

"Influence isn't the word, Tony. I was risking my job just bugging her as much as I did."

"And what does Al Mungo claim? That I wasn't even at his place?"

"No. You were there. You asked him some questions about Sondra Lomax. As it happens, he knows who she is, on account of he owns an interest in the Frenzy Club. But he didn't know the answers."

"Mungo claims I walked into his place under my own steam? No guns at my back?"

"That's right."

"His son, Paul, saw one of Mungo's hoods slap me."

Santini finished his sandwich thoughtfully. "Seems you can't take your liquor, Tony. Mungo offered you a drink. You took it, had a couple more, and suddenly got ugly. Mungo's muscle men were just calming you down."

"How about the girl? Audrey? She saw the way they brought me in. Could you locate her?"

"No trouble. She lives in Mungo's house." Santini made a smacking noise with his lips. *What* a hunk of woman. She ain't just built. She's constructed."

"Did you get your mind off her body long enough to hear what she had to say?"

"She backs Mungo, right down the line."

I finished my coffee, crumpled the container in my fist and hurled it into the wastebasket. "So I just walked into Mungo's, asked a few questions, had a few drinks and walked out."

"Mungo says you wanted more to drink. When he wouldn't give you any more, you got sore. You stomped out saying you'd get your drinks someplace else. Mungo's sorry to hear you got drunk and hurt yourself in a fight."

"And I suppose Mungo's another one with too much influence for you to try squeezing?"

"He's got friends," Santini admitted. "You know I can't push him around just because he used to be in the rackets."

"Pull is what he's got. Not friends. And if he's really retired, I'm Gary Cooper."

Santini shrugged. "A lot of important people like him. He works pretty hard at that respectable-retired-millionaire bit. Donates generously to all the charities. Gives his time to organizations for local betterment. Last month he made a present of a sailboat to the kids in the Palisades Orphanage. He's even chairman of The Florida Committee for the Protection of Homeless Boys. And that outfit's a hobby with some of our best citizens."

"I'll apologize for thinking evil thoughts about Mungo," I said, "the next time I see him."

"You should do that," Santini said, straight-faced. "Al Mungo said to tell you he's really looking forward to meeting you again, under different conditions."

I got the message. The way Mungo saw it, I had ignored his nice little warning by squealing to the cops. He was reminding me of his threat to turn me into a torch.

"So that's the end of it," I said. "First Sondra Lomax, then her roommate. But all you're going to do is look for a guy in a brown suit who happened to be seen running out of Maria Barreto's apartment."

"That's all I can do. I've got absolutely nothing that ties either

Gretchen Forrest or Al Mungo into Maria Barreto's murder. As for Sondra Lomax, there's still nothing to show anything bad happened to her. I contacted the police chief in Las Vegas. He's checking to see if he can locate her. He probably won't, but that doesn't mean anything, either. If she went to Vegas with some guy, she'd likely be checked into some hotel as his wife."

"You don't have to hunt for Sondra Lomax," I told Santini. "She's on a slab in our county morgue."

"So you say. But you haven't given me any evidence." Santini looked at me calmly. "Not yet, you haven't."

"The light dawns," I said slowly. "You're afraid to dig any further, for fear Mungo or Gretchen Forrest'll bring the whole police department down on top of you. So you figure me to do the digging job for you, for free."

"That," Santini admitted, "is the general idea."

"You're not very persuasive."

"I don't have to persuade you. Nothing I could do would *stop* you from doing it, anyway. I've known you a long time, Tony. Since way back when we started together on the force as rookie cops. Nobody ever did you a bad turn that you didn't pay back sooner or later. Like Petrov."

Petrov was an investigator for the district attorney's office. He'd once been an assistant D.A. with bright prospects. Then my father, who'd been a captain in charge of a special squad investigating racketeering, began stepping on too many big toes. Petrov was the one who'd dug up the evidence to put him out of action. He proved that 'way back when my father had been a detective sergeant—and unable to afford the hospital bills for my dying mother—he'd taken a bribe. My father was formally charged. He'd shot himself rather than face me and the trial.

I'd been an armed robbery lieutenant then. I'd quit the department the next day. And found enough of my father's old friends that still liked him and had the influence to get me the license and bond to operate in Florida as a private investigator. The first job I'd done was my own—on Petrov.

"Took you five months," Santini recalled, "to dig up the stuff on Petrov that got him kicked out of the D.A.'s office. And it took him two years and a lot of pull to get back in—even as an investigator. His political future is as dead as your father. Any time he'd try to run for any office, they'd throw that stuff you dug up at him. So that," Santini concluded, "is why I don't have to talk you into doing the dirty work for me now. Mungo had you worked over to stop you. So of course you're not going to stop."

I stood up. "You may end up sorry," I told Santini. "The Department might not like what I dig up. But I warn you right now, nobody's going to sit on any evidence in this case. If it's tried, I'll throw everything I get to the newspaper boys."

It didn't scare him much. He just looked me over and said mildly, "A bit of advice, Tony. First get your strength back. You want to be in condition when you meet up with Mungo's boys again."

9.

I TOOK SANTINI'S ADVICE. You don't snap back in one day after taking that professional a beating. Santini had my car put in a public garage. The fact that I had squealed to the cops told Al Mungo that he hadn't succeeded in scaring me out—that there was only one way I could be stopped. I didn't want my car where any of Mungo's boys would find it—and maybe tamper with it.

I took a cab down to Dinner Key. With all my aches and bruises, it was a rough ride. By the time I climbed aboard the *Straight Pass* and checked through it with the .38 in my hand, I was ready for some more rest.

But not there at the dock. If Mungo was after me, there was only one place where I could sleep with both eyes closed—or even just relax. Out on the water. I started the engines, cast off. I stopped at a supply dock for groceries and ice, then headed for the open sea.

Cruising through the Government Cut, I saw pelicans floating overhead, showing their mossy-green bellies as they scouted for fish. There were dozens of people along the boulders of the breakwater—women sunbathing and inhaling the salty air, men fishing, kids diving off the rocks. There were still a few hours of daylight left.

Which gave me an idea. There was one way I could rest easy

for a day or two and still do a job.

I cut the wheel hard, headed back up into Biscayne Bay.

Half an hour later, I had the *Straight Pass* off the island where Al Mungo and the Forrest sisters lived. I anchored far enough away so that no one on shore would pay me any special attention. Other vessels of all kinds were in the bay. There'd be no reason for anyone to single out my boat as something special.

From my anchoring position I could see both Mungo's place and the Forrest villa through my binoculars. I settled down to watch.

I turned the glasses first on the Forrest place—in time to see Kit Forrest tying up her little catboat at the dock. I watched her take down the sail. She wore a black one-piece bathing suit that set off her long legs and did justice to her slim figure. I raised the binoculars a little, adjusting the screw till I got her face in fine, close focus. She believed herself alone and unobserved, and she looked different that way.

Her features were the same—the bold mouth, the cute nose and large, grave eyes, the delicate-boned beauty of her face. But the self-confidence wasn't there. There was, instead the kind of expression you see in a lonely child contemplating itself in a mirror. Her rich, roan-colored hair was wind-blown, making her look younger than the night before.

After she finished securing the sail, she sat on the end of the dock, facing me, her long, tanned legs dangling over the edge. Her thoughts were turned inward. Then, abruptly, she stood up. The look of cool self-assurance slipped over her face like a mask as she turned and went off the dock, into the house.

I swung the binoculars in a short arc, till I found the pool terrace under the breeze-swayed palms behind Al Mungo's villa. There was a boat tied up at Mungo's dock. It hadn't been there the night before. It was a beautiful sixty-foot cabin cruiser. There was no one in sight aboard it. I raised my glasses a bit.

A pulse jumped in my throat as Al Mungo came into my view.

He was standing near the pool, talking to another man. No one else was around. The man with him was shorter than Mungo, and solidly built. He had the brutal face of the born thug. He wore a rumpled white suit and a straw hat with an orange band.

I wished I could lip-read at that moment. The stocky man seemed to be trying to explain something. Mungo cut him short. His murderous gash of a mouth barely moved when he spoke.

Then Mungo stopped speaking and slapped the other man, backhanding him sharply. It wasn't sudden. You could see it coming as he raised his hand for the swing. But the other man stood there stolidly and awaited it.

Then Mungo hit him again, this time slashing his open palm against the man's other cheek. The straw hat flew off. The man touched his fingers to his face and stood there, waiting for more.

When no more came, he bent down to pick up his straw hat. Mungo kicked him in the stomach.

The man fell on his side, doubled over and clutching at his middle. Mungo gazed down at him coldly. Finally, Mungo's victim rolled over to his knees, found his straw hat, set it back on his head and struggled to his feet.

Mungo spoke again. Whatever he said, it was short and to the point. The thug nodded and hurried away toward the island's inner drive. Mungo stalked off into the house.

I swung the binoculars back to the Forrest place. No one was in sight. I put down the glasses and, going down to the galley, I opened a can of tuna and made myself a sandwich. It felt silly eating canned tuna, with the water full of fresh food. But for once I wasn't sure I'd have the strength to reel in anything I caught.

I had no appetite. But I finished off the sandwich. Then I got a bottle of brandy from the locker in my cabin, and went back up to my chair on the flying bridge. I stayed there till nightfall, alternately sipping brandy and spying on the island.

The soft colors of sunset were in the sky when, having watched the Forrest villa for a time without seeing anyone, I switched back to Mungo's place. At first it seemed that there was no one in sight there, either. Then I saw two people swimming in the pool.

I watched till they climbed out. They were Audrey and Mungo's son, Paul. The bikini the girl wore this time was bright green, but it did as little as the other one to conceal the fabulous opulence of her figure. Paul Mungo, in a pair of elastic swim trunks that showed his lean, lanky build, looked as sullen as ever.

As I watched, they picked up towels and began drying themselves, looking at each other. Then Audrey glanced toward the house. Paul Mungo immediately did the same. Then they looked at each other again. The next instant the space between them was gone. The girl wrapped her arms around Paul's lean waist and their near-nude bodies merged. His fingers crawled into her platinum hair. His face bent to hers.

They parted quickly, almost springing away from each other. Both of them looked again toward the house. Then, walking side by side but not touching, they went into the house together.

***

By the time it was fully dark, the brandy I'd absorbed was overcoming my assorted discomforts and making me sleepy. I went down to my cabin, stretched my tired frame on the bed and was asleep inside two minutes. When I awoke, I lay in darkness for a time, lazily enjoying the fact that I was feeling relatively better. My jaw and temple were still sore, but there was no headache. The worst was my middle, which still ached badly each time I moved. Frenchy and Shev must have concentrated on trying to break me in half after I'd gone out.

I snapped on the bulkhead lamp beside my bed, looked at my watch. I'd been asleep for almost six hours. I continued to lie there for a while. Finally, I got off the bed and went back up to the flying bridge.

The floodlights lit the whole back area of Mungo's place. It was crowded with people having a party all over the terrace, the palm grove and the docked boat. I looked toward the Forrest place. Light showed from inside the house, but that was all.

Lowering myself into the chair again, I took up the binoculars.

Most of the crowd at Mungo's wore bathing suits. Some were in the pool. Those who weren't were drinking and laughing it up. Two Chinese houseboys threaded between clusters of men and women who snatched fresh drinks off the trays they carried.

I spotted Audrey, in a white bikini, surrounded by men. Paul Mungo was one of them. I moved my binoculars from face to face, not finding anyone else I recognized. Until Al Mungo emerged from the house.

He came onto the terrace wearing a green-and-yellow sports shirt and Bermuda shorts that revealed pipe-stem legs. That mouth of his smiled unnaturally as he was greeted happily by several men and women. He drifted toward Audrey.

The men around her made room. He grinned, said something that made them grin—all except his son. Mungo put a possessive hand on the back of Audrey's neck, moved it slowly down her almost-naked back. She arched under his hand, taking it and forcing a smile. Mungo said something again, and the men laughed. Audrey flashed Mungo's son a quick look that beseeched him not to make trouble. I focused on Paul's face. It was a study in fury and misery. He turned away suddenly, jammed his fists in his pockets and slouched off into the house.

Audrey tore her gaze away from where he'd gone, turned her face to Mungo and gave him a quick kiss on the cheek. He grinned, patted her delectable rear, and drifted on.

I kept my binoculars on him. At first there was an apparent aimlessness to the way he wandered from group to group. But soon there was a direction to his wandering that held my attention. Mungo worked his way finally into the palm grove. He stood for a moment on the outer edge of the floodlit area. Then he slipped into the darkness, hurrying along the water's edge in the direction of the Forrest villa.

I switched the binoculars to the Forrest place in time to see a woman emerge from the house. She hesitated for a second on the terrace, her dark, solid figure outlined by the light streaming through the pillars from inside the living room. From her build, I figured it was Gretchen Forrest. She left the terrace, walked quickly down toward the beach.

There, the shadowed figures of Gretchen Forrest and Al Mungo met. They stood together for a full five minutes. Then Gretchen Forrest went back up into her house and Mungo strode along the beach to rejoin his party.

I continued to watch the goings on at that party for a long time, without seeing anything else of special interest. By three in the morning, when the last vestiges of the party had drifted into the house, I made my stiff, aching way back to my cabin, put myself back to sleep with another snifter of brandy.

***

When I found myself wolfing down a second helping of eggs and bacon late the next morning, I knew I was beginning to feel myself. The convincer was that after two hours of watching the island and not seeing anything, a restless impatience gripped me. There were things to be done.

Upping anchor, I started the engines and sailed back down to Dinner Key. But the need for action hadn't robbed me of caution. And it didn't require too much deep thought to figure out why I hadn't spotted Frenchy or Shev at Mungo's place. As I approached Dinner Key, I reversed engines, idled the boat to a slow drift and took up my binoculars.

A long, careful look.

First along my pier. Everything appeared normal. McComb's boat was out, probably a fishing party. The boats that were there belonged.

I studied each of the other piers, one at a time, and the length of the concrete dock. All sorts of people used the piers at Dinner Key. There were entire families who lived on their vessels. There were others who kept their boats there for weekend sailing. There was even a real estate man with a gorgeous ninety-foot schooner-yacht that he used only to impress business contacts. But they all added up to a group with a community feel. After you'd lived there awhile, as I had, you got to know everyone who belonged.

My survey of the piers turned up no one who didn't belong. I raised my binoculars to the parking area behind the dock, studying the cars. That's where I found them.

Frenchy and Shev, sitting in a black Buick sedan.

I put down the binoculars and thought for a moment. Then I worked the throttle and eased the *Straight Pass* into her berth.

10.

THE FIRST THING I DID AFTER CUTTING THE ENGINES was to snub just one line over a pier piling. The second was to get the .38 Special from my cabin and stick it under the belt of my dungarees. I pulled out the bottom of my polo shirt. That way it hid the butt of the .38 but wouldn't interfere with my snatching it up in a hurry.

I made sure of one thing. Shev and Frenchy weren't going to get near enough to put their fists and boots to me again. This time, I figured, it was supposed to go all the way. A kill job.

I kept an eye on the car as I hooked onto the dock lines for the phone, electricity and water supply. Frenchy and Shev stayed where they were, not coming out onto the pier. That didn't surprise me. It was daylight, and there were too many people. They'd tail me till they found a safer place to do it. But I continued to keep a wary watch through the porthole as I changed in my cabin. I put on my dark-blue wash-and-wear suit, slid the .38 into the belt holster under the jacket and went back up to the flying bridge. Frenchy and Shev were still waiting in the black Buick.

I used the binoculars on the license plates. Then I put through a call to the local highway patrol office of the state police.

"I want to report a hit-and-run," I said when I got the dispatcher on the phone. "A black Buick sedan." I gave the license number. "There's two men in it. They ran over a woman on Bay Shore

Drive, south of Grapeland Boulevard, and just kept on going. They're headed north on the Drive."

I repeated the Buick's license number and hung up as the dispatcher began asking for my name.

When I started down the pier, I had my suit jacket draped over my right forearm so that it hid the .38 gripped in my hand. I didn't think they intended to try anything yet. But just in case ... I kept watching their Buick as I reached the end of the pier and followed the curve of the concrete dock till I reached the cab stand.

I got in the back of a cab and told the driver to take me to an East Flagler Street address in downtown Miami.

The driver flipped the meter and drove away from the dock. As the cab turned north onto Bay Shore Drive, I glanced back. Frenchy and Shev were following. Their Buick wouldn't have any trouble catching the cab on the first empty stretch of road we hit.

It came sooner than I'd expected. The long curve of road going past Silver Bluff was deserted.

I gripped the .38 tighter under the jacket as the Buick picked up speed and began to close the gap. Frenchy was driving. The Buick closed in and started a swing that would bring it alongside the cab. I saw Shev raise something and poke it out a little through the open window on his side.

A sawed-off, double-barreled shotgun.

My throat went bone dry. I hadn't figured they'd be so brazen. Suddenly the whine of a siren sounded up ahead. Instantly, the Buick slowed. It slipped back into the lane behind the cab, but kept pace with it. Shev's shotgun vanished.

A state patrol car appeared around the bend of the road ahead, came speeding down the other lane. I watched with a tight grin. The state-police cruiser sirened past us, two watchful cops in the front seat. It was less than a hundred feet past the black Buick when it started to slow down. Another hundred feet and it suddenly made a tight U-turn into our lane, came racing back.

With solid satisfaction, I watched the state cops swing up beside Frenchy and Shev and order them over. It meant about a half-hour delay before the cops made certain my phone call was a hoax. If they happened to take a careful look inside the Buick, and spotted that shotgun, it'd mean more than a half-hour.

I was still looking back through the rear window of the cab when a blue-and-white convertible Chrysler with the top down came speeding into view. It slowed as it passed the Buick and the police car, then kept on at the slower speed, cruising along behind my cab.

I didn't know the blond man driving the convertible, and I was still feeling smug about Frenchy and Shev, so I paid no special attention.

I turned around, relaxed and told the cab driver I'd changed my mind about my destination. I gave him the address of the garage where my car was stashed.

It was a big, white-washed, one-story garage by the river in southeast Miami. I paid the attendant inside what I owed him, got into my Oldsmobile. It was parked up against the rear wall, between a couple pickup trucks belonging to a diaper service. I backed the Olds out from between them, twisting the wheel sharply to avoid backing into a brand-new Cadillac parked behind me. Maneuvering till I got turned around among all the parked vehicles, I headed toward the garage entrance. I braked as I reached the entrance, glanced both ways to check the traffic out in the street.

Something plucked the seat cushion an inch from my right arm.

A spider web of cracks appeared in my windshield. There was a tiny tinkle of the glass breaking, nothing else.

I ducked below the level of the dashboard, grabbing for my .38. There'd been no sound of a shot, which meant that the gun that had fired at me had a silencer on it. That had saved my life. A silencer has its purpose, but it doesn't do your aim any good when your target is some distance away.

Keeping down, I set the hand brake and turned off the ignition. I opened the door at my side and went out of the Olds in a crouch, as fast as I could. Which was pretty fast, considering the aching stiffness of my muscles. I ducked behind the edge of the wall siding the garage entrance, the gun gripped ready in my hand, my finger touching the trigger.

The garage attendant came out of his cubbyhole behind me. "S'matter, mister? Your—" Then he saw the gun in my hand. "Hey! What is—"

"Get back!" I hissed at him.

His eyes went from me to my car, saw the hole in the windshield glass. He was a bright boy. He didn't require diagrams.

I leaned out of the shadows behind the wall, raising the .38. There were a number of buildings across the street, on the bank of the Miami River. There was the looming rear wall of a wholesale seafood storehouse with several windows up high, an abandoned ice factory with shattered windows, a rotting wooden dock with the rusted hulk of an abandoned coastal freighter, a dilapidated rooming house and next to that the side of a big commercial laundry with a dark truck entrance.

The bullet could have been fired from any of those places, but I didn't feel in shape for the kind of stalking job required to find out.

I looked down the length of the street. A long trailer truck was making a slow, tight turn around the corner, heading in my direction.

Crouched low, I got back into my Olds, started the motor and let out the brake. I stayed below the level of the dashboard till the rumbling of the big truck seemed just right. Then I raised my head a little and saw the cab of the truck going past the garage entrance in front of me. I jammed the Olds into gear and drove out into the street, turning into the wrong lane to move side by side with the truck, keeping its trailer between me and the hidden killer across the street.

When we reached the end of the block, I made a sharp turn around the corner, sped for two more blocks till I got into the heavy traffic crossing the Southeast Second Street drawbridge heading into downtown Miami.

I began to breathe easier. But I had enough sense not to get too relaxed again. The fact that the killer must have been waiting for me at that garage meant that Al Mungo must have had every damn public garage and parking lot in the city checked. That was a big job. I'd known Mungo wanted me dead. But I hadn't figured he was in that much of a sweat about it.

I consoled myself with the thought that they weren't likely to try anything at the next place I stopped: the Dade County Courthouse.

I found a parking place opposite the corner of the courthouse, next to the Miami Fire Department's Central Station, where the firemen in their black trousers and white shirts lounged on the benches out front playing checkers and improving their tans. I hurried across the street and up the wide stone steps. At the top, just as I reached the front doors, I did an abrupt turnaround and looked back down.

A blue-and-white Chrysler convertible with the top down was cruising slowly past, a blond-haired man at the wheel.

The same car and driver I'd seen behind my cab after I'd booby-trapped Frenchy and Shev.

The man at the wheel was watching the street ahead of him, not looking my way. When he reached the next corner, I waited for him to make a turn. But he didn't. He kept on going, till he was absorbed from sight in the thick traffic.

It could have been a coincidence.

11.

HAL RUBIN WAS A SKINNY, HIGH-STRUNG TYPE WITH BRIGHT EYES
in a cynical face. It had been an idealistic face, in the days when
I'd first known him. That was back when he'd been new with the
city police.

Now he was in the sheriff's office, and he'd been in on the
arrest—over two years before—of Earl Gronsky, Sondra Lomax's
part-time boyfriend, according to Maria Barreto.

I sat on the edge of Hal's desk and went through the folder.
Gronsky's record went back to his childhood in Jacksonville, and
ranged all over Florida. He'd been a "heavy"—an armed robber—
and he'd always been a lone wolf. He'd been suspected of holding
up everything from dime stores to banks. His list of arrests was
long. But he'd only been convicted twice. Once when he was
eighteen and this last time, when they'd only been able to pin a
minor job on him, a filling-station heist.

He'd been sent to the state prison farm for three years, been
paroled in two. He'd come out of prison earlier that week—on
Tuesday morning.

I looked at the rogues' gallery photos of Earl Gronsky. As I'd
expected, Gronsky was the big man in the brown suit who'd
questioned me at gunpoint in Maria Barreto's apartment.

"They call him the Mad Russian," Hal Rubin remarked.

I closed the folder and slid it across the desk. "Mad-crazy or
mad-angry?"

"Both. He was holed up in a shack in the Everglades off Route Twenty-seven when we got him this last time. I went in after him with six other cops. Caught him sound asleep and no gun. So what's Gronsky do? He comes up off that bed like a volcano and tries to take us apart. All seven of us! And every damn one of us with guns in our mitts. He almost made it out of there, too. Near tore my arm off, throwing me out of his way. A bullet through his shoulder and another in the hip didn't stop him. Heaved one of the boys through that shack wall, planks and all. Knocked two others cold and was kicking the rest away from the door when I finally put him down with my blackjack. I must've hit him with it half a dozen times before he went down."

"He's a pretty big boy, all right," I said.

"Big? He's a monster. And on top of that, he's got nerves of ice. He'd have to, to try some've the things he's pulled. Like holding up big-time gamblers and racket boys."

"That takes guts. Having the cops after you is one thing. Having the mob sore at you's *real* trouble."

"That's so," Rubin admitted, unoffended. "Matter of fact, maybe we did Gronsky a favor when we caught him on that gas-station heist rap. The rumor going around at the time was that Gronsky'd held up a big poker game run by Mike Ryan that same week. Lifted a pot worth a fortune. A lot of it belonging to some racket biggie."

Mike Ryan ran an elusive floating poker game that attracted the heaviest betters in the state. I asked Rubin, "Who was the racket man in the game?"

He shrugged. "Dunno. I do know somebody besides us was supposed to be after him."

"How'd you find out about his hideout in the Everglades?"

"The usual way," Rubin said sarcastically. "An anonymous phone tip."

"And now he's out on parole," I said. "Which means he's got to report his whereabouts and keep in touch. I'd like his present address, Hal."

Rubin looked at me questioningly. But he didn't ask the question. Instead he nodded and said, "I can get it for you, from his parole officer."

"I'll owe you for it."

He used his desk phone to make the call. When he got the address, he scrawled it on a page in his notebook, tore out the page and gave it to me. I glanced at it, stuck it in my pocket. "Mind if I use your phone a minute?"

I put through a call to Lieutenant Santini. "Anything new?"

"Nothing you couldn't fit in a thimble," Santini told me. "The chief in Las Vegas didn't turn up any Sondra Lomax. I checked her hometown. Jacksonville. But she hasn't been in touch with any of her relatives there for years, so they don't know where she is. The Barreto girl doesn't have any relatives living in this country. So we got her in the morgue, too."

I thought about the two girls lying in those cold storage lockers, and felt the gorge rising in me.

"Any luck finding the guy seen running out of Maria Barreto's place?" I asked.

"Nope. How're you making out? Or are you still recuperating?"

"Sort of," I said, and hung up.

I told Hal Rubin, "Thanks for the time and trouble."

"S'all right. I only got about three million other things to do."

I stood up, thought of something else. "Ever heard of a Larry Score?"

He didn't have to think it over. "Sure. He's Al Mungo's number-one boy. A really ugly one. I don't mean his looks. Matter of fact he's a pretty handsome boy. Young, blond, looks like an actor or something. But he's pure murder with a gun or a knife. Not," Rubin added angrily, "that we've ever been able to pin a murder on him."

"He suspected of any?"

"Any?" Rubin blurted. "There's *five* I'd swear on my mother's grave he did. Gang execution jobs."

I said thanks again, and left Rubin's office.

Going along the corridor to the windows at the front end, I looked out. I didn't have to do much searching. The blue-and-white convertible was parked on the same side of the street as my car.

The blond man sat behind the wheel smoking a cigarette. He was partially turned around in the seat, watching the entrance of the courthouse.

I went back down the corridor to the men's room. When I came out, I had my jacket draped carefully over my forearm again.

By the time I crossed the street and reached my Olds, the blond in the convertible was turned around with the back of his head toward me.

I strolled on past my car, stopped when I reached his. I put my left hand on the top of the door beside him and said, "Hello, Larry. Sorry to've kept you waiting."

It flustered him for a second. Then he got a blank look and gave it to me. "You drunk or something, bud?"

He was a handsome boy all right. And smooth. His blond hair was crew-cut, giving him that boyish look that went with his clean-chiseled features and the lean strength of his build. But there was nothing young about his pale gray eyes. A cobra would have been proud of the expression in those eyes. I guessed that it was that combination of boyish prettiness and the dangerous look that turned the girls to mush.

"How's old Al Mungo holding up?" I asked, and suddenly darted my left hand down inside the car and snatched the key from the ignition.

Larry Score went for the gun in the shoulder holster that bulged the front of his sports jacket. I said "No," and raised my right hand, showing him the snout of the gun under the jacket. His hand froze, his fingertips just touching his lapel.

"Hands on the wheel," I said softly.

He did it. But then he began to recover a little from the shock. He tried a sneer. "You know damn well you can't use a gun on me here."

"I don't know it," I assured him. "Any more than you do. Why don't you try something, and we'll both find out."

We stared at each other. My stare was more effective. I had a gun to help.

He had been quite right, of course. I wasn't about to gun anybody down on busy Flagler Street, half a block from the courthouse, in broad daylight. But Al Mungo's number-one boy didn't quite have the sand to call my bluff.

I didn't blame him. He didn't know me. I might be just crazy enough—or frightened enough—to squeeze that trigger.

Okay, I said softly, dropping his ignition key in my pocket and opening the car door. "Slide over."

"What?"

"You can hear. Don't make me nervous."

Larry Score slid over. I got in beside him and shut the door. Holding the .38 on my thigh, aimed at his stomach, I told him, "Put your hands on your knees."

He did. He stared straight ahead through the windshield and whispered, "You don't have to worry about me ever gunning you, Rome. Not anymore. When I get you it'll be a slow knife job."

"Convenient of you to show up," I said. "I've been wanting a talk with you. What happened to Sondra Lomax?"

"Did something happen to her?" he asked coolly.

"She doesn't seem to be around anymore."

"She went to Las Vegas," Larry Score said negligently.

"I thought Sondra was supposed to be your girl."

Score shrugged. "I got lots of girls. And anyway, I ain't been' making the scene with Sondra lately. I got a new broad."

"You took Sondra to Gretchen Forrest's party Tuesday night."

"No, I didn't. Gretchen was my date. It was Danny Yale took Sondra along."

"What time did Yale and Sondra leave the party?"

"They didn't. Sondra cut out early. Danny stuck." Larry Score looked at me. "You know, you're making a lot of trouble over nothing."

"Who'd Sondra leave the party with?"

"Who knows? I was busy. I didn't see."

"Who's this guy Sondra went to Las Vegas with?"

"I don't know. Gretchen's the jealous kind."

"Gretchen," I said," should have better taste in men."

He grinned. "She knows what she likes."

"Yeah, I heard you were a lady-killer. Man-killer, too. How's it pay?"

"I get along."

"So far," I said. "Now untie your shoelaces."

"Huh?"

"Your shoelaces."

Puzzled, Larry Score bent down to pull at his shoelaces. I leaned over and chopped the base of his skull with the heavy butt of my gun.

Not hard enough to put him out cold. That would have required too much of a swing of my arm, and someone passing by might have seen what I was doing. This way it just stunned him, which was enough. His shoulders sagged between his spread knees; I rearranged my jacket over the .38, grabbed the back of his collar with my left hand and pulled him up to a sitting position.

His body slumped sideways a little. His groggy head lolled on the seat cushion. He covered his glazed eyes with his hands and groaned. I got out of the car and shut the door.

A man stopped beside me, looking worried. "What happened? Is he . . . ."

"Sick," I said. "I've got to get a doctor."

I hurried back to my car, got it started, made a tight, fast U-turn that got me headed west, and drove off. Going over the Flagler Street drawbridge, I tossed Larry Score's ignition key into the Miami River.

In a way, it had been like warming up with a sparring partner before climbing into the ring with the champ. Next stop was the big man in the brown suit. Alias the Mad Russian.

12.

IT WAS OUT ALONG THE RAILROAD FREIGHT SIDINGS in northwest Miami. A neighborhood of mammoth junk yards and metal processing plants, with some isolated juke bars, diners, ramshackle boarding houses and concrete-block cabins squeezed in among them. The whole area reverberated with noise—the smashing of scrap metal being compressed into solid blocks, the chugging of freight cars, the crashing of metal being dumped aboard them.

This was one of the concrete-block cabins, with a rusty corrugated tin roof. It was behind a clapboard diner that squatted beside the tracks. The other three sides of the cabin faced the blank walls of a steel-pipe factory, a lead products storehouse and an aluminum-processing plant. Sprawled between these and the distant street, and looming high above them, were huge mountains of scrap. The harsh smells of rust and acrid smoke from metal-melting furnaces stayed with me as I made a cautious approach to Earl Gronsky's cabin. I was carrying my jacket to conceal the gun in my hand again. It was getting to be a habit. But I didn't feel silly about it. Not tackling Gronsky I didn't.

I approached from the rear, warily sidling along the concrete-block wall to peek through the single window there. I looked into a room that took up most of the cabin. There was a kitchen table and some unpainted wooden chairs. Against one wall was an ancient bureau with a two-burner electric cooker. Against the opposite wall was a narrow, unmade bed. Otherwise, the room was empty.

There was a closed door that might lead to a closet or a small bathroom. Walking around to the front of the cabin, I knocked at the door. There was no response. I went back and looked through the window again. The inside door was still closed.

Going into the clapboard diner, I took a stool at one end of the plank counter that gave me a view of the approaches to the cabin. I ordered lamb stew, with coffee, and took my time. I was mopping up the gravy when the factory whistles tooted and men finished working began crowding in.

I walked back through the metal plants and the scrap yards till I reached the street and my Oldsmobile. I got the flask of brandy from the glove compartment and had some, then sat behind the wheel for a while. But as a lookout post it wasn't good enough. I couldn't see all the approaches to Gronsky's cabin. He might come across the railroad tracks on the other side. It was getting murky with dusk, so I found a vantage spot between the aluminum plant and the steel pipe factory.

The long, restless waiting sessions were a part of my job that I had never learned to like. But I had learned to live with them. I waited. The owner of the diner locked up for the night and went home. Night closed in, and the whole area filled with deserted darkness. Not a light anywhere.

My various aches and bruises began to protest. I decided I might as well wait in reasonable comfort. Making my way back to the rear of the cabin, I tried the window. It was locked. Using the muzzle of my .38, I poked a hole in one of the panes of glass. I pushed the barrel of the gun through the hole and worked the lock open. Pulling up the window, I climbed over the sill.

The sun had been baking down on that tin roof all day, and the cabin held the heat like a closed oven. I left the window open for a while, till some of the night air from outside had thinned the stuffiness. Then I shut the window and felt my way to the closed inner door. I opened it and lighted a match for a look. It was a small bathroom. Just a sink and a toilet, nothing else. Closing the door, I felt my way across the room to the narrow bed. I stretched out with my gun in my hand.

I wasn't afraid of falling asleep. The thought of Gronsky walking in on me kept me too keyed up for that. But after another hour dragged by, I began to think I'd made a mistake. The hot, heavy air got to be more than I could take. I was making up my mind to get out when I heard a key in the lock.

I sat up fast, swinging my feet to the floor and leveling my gun.

The door swung open, and his shadowy bulk loomed through it. He flicked the wall switch. A single bare bulb in the ceiling went on, shedding yellowish light around the room.

He looked even bigger and meaner than I'd remembered. I stood up, but he still made me feel like a midget. He looked at me and my gun and a thoughtful frown came over his big-featured face. The big diamond on his little finger glinted as he raised his left hand and scratched his ear. "Wha'd'ya know," he murmured. He looked around, then back to me. "Just you?"

"Just me," I said. "Like the last time. Only in reverse. Me with the gun and the questions. You with the answers."

He said "Wha'd'ya know" again. The gun I was pointing at him didn't seem to impress him much. I couldn't think of many things that would impress a guy with his size and swift, destructive power. The image of big Frenchy jumped into my mind. The thought of Frenchy tangling with Gronsky was a pleasant one. Gronsky would have made hamburger out of Mungo's pet football player.

"Open your jacket," I ordered Gronsky.

He thought about it. Then, as though he could think of no objection, he unbuttoned his jacket and flipped it open, revealing the .45 automatic in the holster under his arm.

"Take out the gun," I told him. "With just your fingertips." I was wound tight as a steel spring inside. The sweating I was doing wasn't all from the heat.

The Mad Russian grinned at me. "Why'n't you come take it off me, pal?"

"If you're trying to scare me." I said, "you don't have to work at it much. I'm scared, and my finger's on this trigger. Think about that." I let him hear the jumpiness in my voice.

He considered it for a moment. Then, with the tips of his thumb and forefinger, he removed the .45 from his holster, held it and looked at me coolly.

"Toss it this way," I snapped.

He tossed it. The automatic bounced on the bed behind me. I breathed a little easier. Just a little. Gronsky looked relaxed. But he wasn't. I could feel the tension in him, I could feel him holding back his strength till I made any slip that gave him a chance to use it.

"Hot in here," he said suddenly, and strode across the room to the rear window. He tugged it open wide from the bottom. "That's more like it." He turned and looked at me again, grinning wolfishly.

"You know, pal," he said conversationally, "busting into my place like you did's illegal. Even the real cops'd need a warrant. And you're just a private dick. Could get you in a lot of trouble."

"Sure," I agreed. "You go to the cops and complain. They'd be real happy about it. They've been looking for you hard enough."

He frowned again. "Looking for me? Why? I'm out clean. I ain't done nothing yet."

"They think you killed Maria Barreto."

"The Spanish dish in Sondra's apartment?"

"Uh huh."

"Wasn't me that did it. I didn't touch her. Never even got to talk to her."

"You were seen running out of her place, leaving her dead."

"She was that way when I got there," Gronsky told me. "I went up to ask her did she know where Sondra is. I knocked, but nothing happened. The door wasn't locked, so I went in. And seen the way she was. So I got out fast."

"You'll play hell trying to make the cops believe you."

Gronsky eyed me shrewdly. He might have been mad, but he wasn't dumb. "So if the fuzz're after me, how come they ain't here? My parole officer's got my address."

"They don't know your name. Just what you look like. I didn't tell them who the description fitted."

"How come?"

"I don't figure you killed her," I said. "I think she was rubbed on orders from Al Mungo. You're not a mob boy. You've always been strictly a loner. And killing for hire's not your line."

Face furrowed with concentration, Gronsky lowered his bulk to one of the wooden chairs. He scratched his ear again. "You know a lot about me. And you ain't one've Mungo's poodles, or you wouldn't't've come after me all by yourself. So how come you know so much?"

"I looked you up. I think you've got some answers that might help me work something out."

"Yeah? Something like what?"

I sat in a chair facing him, but keeping the distance between us. "A couple murders I'd like to pin on Al Mungo. I've got a grudge to settle with him. Maybe you do, too?"

He gave a short laugh. "Not me. It's the other way 'round." Then his grin went away and he said, "But I'll tell you one thing. *I* sure didn't squeeze that Spanish girl. Why would I? It's Sondra I wanna get my hands on."

"Why?"

"Why d'you think? The double-crossing bitch squealed on me to the law. Told 'em where to find me. I just finished spending two lousy years in the can on account've her."

"How do you know it was her?" I asked him.

"It was her all right. Sondra was the only one knew where I was holed up. Nobody else."

"You've been hunting for her boat, too," I said. "Why?" Gronsky's eyes narrowed, reappraising me. "It's mine. I gave it to her. Then she goes and plays me for a sucker. I want it back. I got a use for it. What makes it your business?"

"I think I know where it is. Help me figure out how it fits in, and maybe we can make a deal."

"Fits in what?" Gronsky demanded, puzzled. Then he stood up.

He did it so suddenly it took me by surprise. I knocked over my chair jumping up. "Easy," I warned, raising the .38 a little.

"All of a sudden I don't know about you," he said heavily. "Mungo could be playing it cute. He knows *he* couldn't get anything out of me. So he sicks you onto me to—"

"You know better," I told him. "You read about me in the paper. You know how I got into this."

"Maybe. Okay, you tell me. Where's the boat?"

"Show your cards first."

He looked me up and down, slow. "I guess I got to bust it out've you."

"Think again. It's my deal."

"Says which?"

"This gun."

"That? Take more'n a little ol' .38 slug to stop me, pal."

He took a step toward me. "Hold it," I rasped desperately. "I don't *want* to plug you."

"Better not," Gronsky warned. "It'd make me sore." I saw his gigantic frame braced to jump me.

There was a knock at the front door of the cabin.

We both switched around to stare at the door.

A hard voice behind us whispered, "Get your hands up! Empty."

I twisted my head and saw the .357 Magnum pointing in through the open window at us—saw the hawk-faced man holding it. I opened my hand and let the .38 thud to the floor. I put my hands above my head.

Earl Gronsky wasn't so quick about it He looked toward the window, thinking it over.

"Don't be stupid, Gronsky," the hawk-faced man said. "This ain't no .38 I'm holding on you. A Magnum slug'll blow a hole in you big enough to put a fist through."

Gronsky slowly raised his massive arms.

"Okay, Terry!" the hawk-faced man called out.

The door of the shack opened. In came the heavy-set, brutal-faced man in the white suit and straw hat. The one I'd watched take Al Mungo's slaps and kicks, then scurry off to do his bidding. He was carrying a Magnum, too. Mungo's boys obviously all liked their artillery heavy and certain.

"Well, well," Gronsky said softly. "If it ain't Terry Kay. I saw you waiting with this other jerk when I come outa the can Tuesday. Thought I gave you the slip."

"You did, you bastard. And I got the lumps for it. It's gonna be a pleasure to watch you get yours."

The hawk-faced one had climbed in the windows. "Who the hell are you?" he demanded, pointing the heavy gun at me.

"I just happened to drop in," I said.

Gronsky looked at me and said, "Guess I was right about you the first time. Sorry, pal."

"I asked you something," Hawk-face reminded me thinly.

"What's it matter?" Kay snapped. "Whoever he is, we can't just leave him behind."

"We can leave him dead," Hawk-face said casually. "Nobody around to hear the shot."

Kay considered it.

"*I'll* do it," Hawk-face said, "if you don't wanna. No trouble at all that way. Bing. In the head. Then we don't hafta worry about him." He smiled at me.

"Maybe we better take him along," Kay mused. "Let Mungo decide."

"Mungo didn't say nothing about bringing anybody else," Hawk-face pointed out. "Just Gronsky."

"He didn't say anything about killing a guy we don't even know, either."

"What the hell would he care?" Hawk-face said. "Just another guy dead. And nothing to tie his body to us."

"We better leave it to Mungo," Kay insisted, suddenly decisive. "That way he can't claim I loused something up again."

Hawk-face gave in. "Okay. But it just means more work for us."

I breathed again.

Hawk-face reached into his pocket with his free hand and drew out a blackjack. He motioned at Gronsky and me with his Magnum. "Turn around. Backs to me."

"No," Kay said. "Wait'll we reach the car. Knock 'em out here 'n' we got to carry 'em all that way."

Hawk-face shrugged, dropped the blackjack back in his pocket. Kay edged over to the bed, doing it so that he continued to face us. With his free hand, he picked up Gronsky's .45, stuffed it in his pocket. Then he squatted, straightened with my' .38 in his left hand, his Magnum in his right. He pointed both guns at us. "You go first," he told Hawk-face.

Hawk-face backed to the doorway, stopped there with his gun ready.

"Now you two," Kay ordered. Gronsky murmured softly to me, "Stay loose, pal." He turned and started for the door. Hawk-face backed out as he approached. I followed Gronsky. Kay came behind me, keeping out of arm's reach.

Outside the cabin there was just enough moonlight to see each other by. The boys with the guns took up positions behind us— Kay off to Gronsky's left, Hawk-face off to my right

"March," Kay ordered.

Gronsky and I started walking, side by side, following Kay's quiet directions. I tried to stay loose, the way Gronsky had said. But it was hard, thinking of those guns aimed at my back. Knowing where those guns were taking me. And what would be done to me after we got there.

We walked in the direction of the street, going between the walls of two of the metal-products plants. The scrap piles rose ahead, dark hills against the night sky. We trudged into the heavily shadowed valley between a mound of wrecked automobiles rearing as high as a three-story house and an enormous pile of rusting, twisted girders, bedsprings, hot water tanks and old-fashioned bathtubs. In that valley, Gronsky, walking close beside me, became a vague, dark shadow.

The shadow swung out a hand and poked a thick finger into my arm. I tensed, setting myself for it.

But even so, his move, when it came, was so fast that it caught me in mid-stride and I almost didn't react in time.

He suddenly bent low, spun around and launched himself at Kay. I twisted around as one of the guns in Kay's fists roared and spurted flame. The slug went over Gronsky, whipped past my cheek, and clanged into the mountain of smashed automobiles behind me. The next instant Gronsky had Kay—one hand around his throat, the other gripping a leg. Kay screamed wildly as Gronsky heaved him up high above his head and hurled him with incredible force at Hawk-face. Hawk-face leaped aside just in time. Kay's flailing figure somersaulted past him and crashed into the pile of scrap metal, bounced off it and sprawled to the dark ground.

The Magnum in Hawk-face's hand boomed as Kay fell. Gronsky's right leg snapped back. His giant figure toppled face down between us. I went off my feet in a headlong dive over Gronsky. Kay didn't stir when I landed on top of him. My hands scrambled frantically, fingers searching for his pocket. Hawk-face's second shot tugged the cloth of my jacket as I found the pocket and dragged Gronsky's .45 out. I thumbed off the safety and rolled off Kay as I blasted a snap shot at Hawk-face. The deeply shadowed darkness that had saved me from his shot saved him from mine. The slug rang twice as it bounded off metal. But it was enough to make Hawk-face jump backward through the shadows. The next instant he vanished behind the mountainous uprearing of wrecked cars.

I came up on my knees and stayed there for a few moments with the .45 gripped in my perspiring fingers, breathing fast and straining to see through the shadows. I moved my left hand over Kay, stopped when I reached his neck. It had been broken by the force of Gronsky's throw.

"Gronsky?" I hissed.

"I'm still here," he whispered back. "But that's all for me. Near tore my leg off. Bones're busted." His voice betrayed no trace of the agony he must have been feeling. "You better get that bastard," he said, "or he'll get us."

"Can you move?" I asked, hunting nervously for a glimpse of anything moving around that mountain of automobiles.

"Yeah. A little. Dragging."

"Move then," I told him. "He knows where you are."

"You, too," Gronsky whispered back.

I nodded, though he couldn't see the nod in the darkness. Getting my feet under me, I moved forward in a low crouch, testing each step so that I made no sound. I reached the mountain of tangled cars, waited and listened. I heard nothing. I looked quickly to my left, then my right. Nothing appeared to be moving in the shadows around the base of that fantastic pile of vehicles.

I started around it, moving to my right. Then I stopped. Hawk-face was probably waiting for me around the other side. He might be near, or some distance away—or even up in one of the cars.

I looked at the jumble looming over me. At the bottom of the pile, in front of me, was an old Cadillac, upside down. Getting a foot up on its axle and seizing one of its tireless wheels with my left hand, I pulled myself up in among the cars, wriggled between the wheels of a truck resting on the Cadillac. I crawled over the smashed-in roof of another car, climbed the tilted side of still another, made my way around a squashed-in hood and squeezed myself between the understructures of two automobiles standing upright with their wheels crunched together.

They say that people going into the interior of an Egyptian pyramid get a nightmarish feeling that all the thousands of slaves who died building it are there, observing them. I began to experience much the same sensation inside that mountain of automobiles. Few of the cars were ancient. Most were there as a result of accidents so severe that they had value now only as junk.

Each was a separate story of disaster, of people dead or horribly maimed. In the silence of the metal mountain's interior I seemed to hear the ghostly distant violence of skidding tires, screaming passengers, screeching tires, crashing metal; the sobbing of mangled victims.

I worked past a car whose engine had been driven back through the front seat, one whose roof had been flattened down on both seats, another twisted into the shape of a horseshoe, one whose gas tank had caught fire and burned the interior upholstery to ashes.

It was slow, delicate work. I reached the heart of the bottom of the pile of automobiles, drenched with perspiration. But worse than that was the dizzying fear. All that had to happen was for my weight to move any one of those cars—just a little. Then the whole mountain around and above me would settle and squash me to jelly. Conscious every inch of the way of those hundreds of tons pressuring downward above me, I dragged myself carefully on through twisting, tortured tunnels of junk.

A sports car, smashed almost beyond recognition, blocked the end of one of those tunnels. And there was no room for me to turn around. I was forced to drag myself backward, feet first, searching for a detour.

The cuff of my trouser leg snagged on a shredded fender behind me. Hemmed in by car doors pressing against my shoulders and a blown-out tire touching the small of my back, I couldn't reach my trapped leg with either hand. Cautiously, I worked my leg, trying to extricate it. I couldn't. The material of my trousers was caught like the mouth of a fish on a barbed hook. Finally, sucking in a deep breath to hold back panic, I started to pull my leg up, slowly, steadily. I heard the tearing of cloth, and then my leg was free. Nothing in that pile of automobile corpses shifted. I let out my breath.

I began wriggling backward again. Reached the side of an old Studebaker. Catching hold of its door handle, I hauled myself up, climbed in through its window into the gutted front seat. Climbed out the other window under the hanging wheels of another car.

Reassessing my direction, I crawled to my left, went through the open, engineless hood of a truck cab.

I suddenly found myself looking out into the junk yard on the other side of the automobile pile.

I lay still, hardly breathing. I saw nothing that moved. I waited, the .45 gripped in my hand.

Then I heard something below me. The scrape of shoe leather against the ground.

I pointed the .45 straight down and fired blindly, the shot blasting the night stillness.

One of the shadows moved, leaping away from the foot of the pile. There was a flash of gunfire and the Magnum's boom. Hawk-face's heavy slug chewed metal inches above my head. I fired twice in rapid succession at his gun flash, squeezing the trigger and feeling the automatic roar and recoil in my hand.

Hawk-face jumped toward a mound of scrap metal, triggering shots at me as he ran, his bullets clanging among the cars all around me. Then, for an instant, the moonlight caught him, starkly outlining his dark figure. I aimed quickly and shot him, saw the bullet slam him against the pile of junk. He bounced off it, stumbled a couple steps and blasted another shot in my direction. The slug rang against metal below my face as I shot him again. My bullet knocked him off his feet, spun him around in midair and dropped him to the ground like a bag of loose bones.

I dragged myself out of the automobile pile, climbed down its slope to the ground, sprinted toward Hawk-face in a low crouch, the .45 in my hand ready for another shot. It wasn't needed. My first shot had torn his side. The second had smashed through his ribs and stopped his heart.

Dragging gulps of air into my lungs, I hurried back to where I'd left Gronsky. He wasn't there. I called his name.

"Here," he called back weakly.

I found him lying on the ground between a bathtub and a rusty boiler. His right leg was stretched out at an unnatural angle, blood soaking the trouser leg from above the knee down to the cuff. His shoe was wet with it. He'd taken off his necktie and tied it around his thigh as a tourniquet.

"Get him?" Gronsky rasped.

"Got him. Wait here." I went to where Kay was, felt around his body till I found my .38. Sticking the .45 in my left jacket pocket and the .38 in my right, I went back to Gronsky.

"Got to get outa here," he whispered shakily. "Anybody heard those shots, the law'll be on its way. I know a guy'll hide me."

"It's a hospital you need," I told him.

"I ain't taking any rap for a murder I didn't do," he growled.

I wasn't in a mood for arguing. "Let's see if we can get you to my car."

I helped him sit up. A low groan escaped his clenched teeth, but he got his right arm over my shoulders.

"Use me like a crutch," I said. We started slowly past the piles of scrap toward the street, Gronsky hanging onto me and hopping on his left foot.

We had managed to progress maybe twenty feet when two flashlights suddenly snapped on and caught us in their glare.

I let go of Gronsky and snatched the .38 from my pocket.

"Hold it," a harsh voice barked. "You're covered. Drop that gun!"

Then I saw the shine of brass buttons behind the flashlights.

Gronsky, sitting on the ground beside me, saw too.

"Cops," he growled disgustedly. "That tears it."

I dropped my gun. The two cops moved in on us, their guns out. I told them quickly who and what I was. "You can check me out with Lieutenant Santini in City Homicide, or Hal Rubin in the sheriff's office."

"We'll see," one of the cops said. He got the .45 from my pocket, bent and picked up my .38, patted Gronsky for weapons. He straightened, said to the other cop, "We better call this in fast."

Each of them took one of Gronsky's arms and lifted him. I was ordered to walk ahead toward the street. Taking it slow, we reached the pavement where the police car was parked in front of my Olds.

"Here," one of the cops said as they helped Gronsky hop to the side of their car, "we'll settle you in the back seat and—"

Gronsky's arms, held across their shoulders, suddenly moved. Balancing on his left leg, he jerked his wrists out of their hands. Before they realized what was happening, Gronsky had gripped their necks with his powerful fingers and was throwing both of them at me.

One of the cops stumbled a few steps, then caught his balance. The other one crashed into me and we both went down on the pavement. Gronsky hurled himself into the front seat of the police car, behind the wheel. He was snapping on the ignition when the cop who was still on his feet leaped to the open car door and swung his nightstick. It caught Gronsky on the temple, knocked him over sideways in the front seat.

He bounced back up like he was made of springs. His head lolled drunkenly on his thick neck, but his huge hands reached out for the cop's throat. The cop swung the night stick again, slamming it down on the top of Gronsky's noggin with all his strength.

For a second, Gronsky seemed not to have felt it. He sat there, his hands still stretched out toward the cop. Then his eyes glazed. He toppled forward out of the car, smacked the pavement face down and lay still.

The cop with the night stick stood over him, breathing hard and looking dumbfounded.

"What a man!" he whispered.

13.

I PUT IN A ROUGH SESSION IN THE HEADQUARTERS office of Captain Murray Jones. There were four of us—myself, Captain Jones, Al Mungo and Mungo's lawyer. But Mungo's lawyer, an ex-D.A. who was now the most respected criminal attorney in the state, did most of the talking. Mungo didn't say a word. He just didn't take his eyes off me the whole time. Lamplight glittered against his horn-rimmed glasses and masked the expression in his eyes. But his gash of a mouth carried all the expression I needed to get the message.

What his lawyer had to say added up to the indisputable fact that I couldn't prove any of the charges I'd made. There was no proof that Mungo had had me beaten, or was trying to have me killed. No proof that I'd seen Kay at Mungo's place, or that Kay or Hawk-face—both known hoodlums who'd worked for anybody with the price—were in any way connected with Mungo.

Captain Jones didn't like it much, but he was forced to agree.

"And," Mungo's lawyer concluded, glaring at me righteously, "if there is just one more instance of your making unsubstantiated charges against my client, we'll take *you* to court. Consider yourself fortunate if the worst that happens to you is the loss of your license. Understand?"

I understood.

After Mungo and his lawyer left, Captain Jones gave me a mild-voiced lecture. He didn't go for Mungo any more than I did. Men who got rich on vice and murder, and then figured they could buy respectability, made his blood pressure soar. The lawyers who helped such men maintain their respectable facades turned his stomach. But without proof, the letter of the law was on Mungo's side. And between them, Mungo and his lawyer had the influence to make the sky fall in on me.

Outside Jones's office, his police secretary had ready the typed-up statement I'd made about the night's occurrences. I signed it, found Santini, and the two of us went to pay a call on Earl Gronsky in the hospital.

The Mad Russian was all out of luck. The deaths of Kay and Hawk-face had automatically brought Homicide into it. Lieutenant Santini had taken one look at Gronsky's size and the brown suit he still wore, and called in his witness from the apartment below Maria Barreto's. The woman had identified Gronsky as the man she'd seen running out of the dead Barreto girl's place.

Gronsky, charged with strangling Maria to death, had shut up like a clam. All they'd been able to get him to say was that he wanted to see me.

Gronsky had a room to himself at the hospital, with a cop guarding him. Only one cop. But they figured that Gronsky, with his leg smashed, splinted and up in traction, wasn't going to be much of a problem. I wasn't so sure. Even flat on his back on his bed, with his leg tied up in the pulleys, he looked formidable. He had his head propped up by two pillows and was smoking a cigarette when we entered his room.

When he saw me, he snubbed the cigarette out in the ashtray on his chest and said, "Hi, pal. How'd you do?"

"Better than you."

"You're out clean?"

"Uh huh. Those two hoods had records as messy as your leg. Nobody seems to regret their loss."

"Okay, then," Gronsky said. "I got a proposition. You're a

private dick. I want you should do a job for me. They're pinning a bum rap on me. Get me out of it."

Santini's jawline tightened. "If it's a bum rap, try being honest with us for a change. That's the way to prove you're innocent. Start opening up and—"

"Nuts!" Gronsky said. "The law'd just use every word I said to sew me up more."

"Rome isn't likely to turn up anything we can't," Santini snapped.

"It's what he uses it for that makes the difference," Gronsky said. "You ain't for *me*. The law works for the law. Rome works for money. If it's my money, he'll be working for me."

Gronsky pulled the big diamond ring off the little finger of his left hand, held it up to the light. "See this? You can get fifteen hundred bucks for it, any place. I know. Had to hock it a couple times."

He tossed the ring at Santini, who caught it with both hands. "Check it out, Lieutenant," Gronsky told him. "It ain't hot. It's mine, legal. Bought it three years ago from the Mayfair jewelry store, over on the Beach."

He looked at me again. "It's yours, when you prove I didn't kill the Barreto girl. The lieutenant here's your witness I say so."

I considered it. "All right, it's a deal. But understand one thing. If I turn up evidence that you did kill her, I won't smother it. It'll go to the cops to help make their case against you."

"I didn't kill her," Gronsky said, his voice tired. "Prove it and get the law off my back, and the ring's yours. Otherwise, I got to use it to buy me a smart lawyer."

***

I checked into a Biscayne Boulevard hotel under a false name for the rest of that night. Mungo's death sentence was still on me. I didn't want to go anywhere his executioners might be waiting. I had a double brandy sent up to my room and used it to soothe my shredded nerves till sleep came.

I felt better the next morning. The effects of what Frenchy and Shev had done had subsided. After breakfast I got a shave, then went to a department store and bought a change of clothes. I needed a new suit anyway, after that crawl through the heap of wrecked cars. I changed and put in a call to my office. Margo said that there'd been a call for me a few minutes after nine that morning. From Gretchen Forrest. She wanted me to contact her at once.

I looked up her number and put the call through from a phone booth.

"Mr. Rome," she said when she came on the phone, "I have to talk to you."

"About what?"

"I want to hire you. It's—it's something I can't talk about over the phone."

"All right," I told her. "Can you be at my office in about an hour?" I gave her the address.

"I'd rather you came here," Gretchen Forrest said. "I'll pay for your time. And it'll be just as easy for us to talk here."

"Yeah. But not so safe."

"What?"

"I don't like some of your neighbors, Miss Forrest. My office. In an hour." I hung up on her.

My visit to the Coast Guard didn't take long. I only wanted to check out Maria Barreto's story about the boat. It checked. The accident had been duly recorded, its location marked on the Coast Guard charts according to regulations.

The boat owned by one Sondra Lomax had been a twenty-two-foot Fiberglass cabin skiff powered by two outboards. It had torn its keel on a submerged rock off Elliot Key and sunk. No casualties.

I made a thorough check of the neighborhood around my office building before entering. There was no sign of Mungo's boys, which puzzled me. When I made my wary way up to my office and into it without running into an ambush, I became still more puzzled. Closing my office door, I checked the closet. Nothing there but my raincoat.

I sat in the swivel chair behind my desk and thought. Then I put my .38 Special in the middle drawer of the desk, left the drawer open just enough to be able to get it out in a hurry. I waited.

You can't tell much from the shadow of a person through frosted glass. There was a knock. I put my hand on the gun. "Come in."

It was Gretchen Forrest. She was wearing a light-green suit tailored neatly to her buxom figure. There didn't seem to be anyone else. She closed the door behind her.

"Would you please lock it," I suggested.

"Lock it?"

"I don't want anyone disturbing us. I assume you feel the same."

She turned the lock. I let go of the gun and took my hand my out of the drawer. "Have a seat, Miss Forrest."

She was a lot more self-possessed than the last time. And sober. First she glanced around my office with a look that pegged my income bracket Her guess was wrong, but then she didn't know how much I spent to feed the gambling fever. She came to my desk and sat down erect on the leather chair beside it. She stripped off her olive-green gloves and arranged them neatly on top of the handbag on her knees. Then she looked at me again.

That upset her a little. That close-up look. I reached up a hand and touched fingers to the tenderness under my left eye. The swelling there and along my jaw was gone, and the lump on my temple was down. But the bruises still showed.

"Souvenir from your friends," I told her.

"I'm sorry. Did they hurt you very much?"

"They hurt me."

"Well—I *am* sorry." She repeated it defiantly. She wasn't used to saying it, and she resented my putting her in that position. "That's why I had to see you. To explain, and . . . ." She hesitated, studying me almost angrily. "Can I trust you?"

"With what?"

"Certain—facts about me."

"I've had this office quite a while," I told her. "Private detectives who can't be trusted don't last long. Word gets around."

She thought about that. Then she said fiercely, "It's all that lousy money my father made, of course. All it's ever bought me is trouble. Starting with that horrible custody fight over me and Kit after my father died. I was only thirteen then, but I've never forgotten a single lousy little detail of it. That's one of the things Kit has been spared. She was only a baby."

Her head came up and her face tightened with an angry, defensive pride. "Kit's been spared a *lot* of things that I haven't. Sometimes I think Kit's spent her life just watching what happened to me, and then walking around every pitfall she's seen me fall into."

She became silent. I lit a Lucky, waited for her to continue.

"Mind if I have that?" Gretchen Forrest asked, holding out a hand. "I'll bet I need it more than you do."

I took the cigarette from my lips and gave it to her. She put it between her lips and took a drag, let the smoke curl out of her mouth and looked at me narrow-eyed through it. It was an intimate gesture. But she did it too smoothly, too expertly. I could feel all the times she'd used the gimmick, all the men she'd used it on.

"You know," she murmured, "you are a very attractive man, Mr. Rome. I *am* sorry they damaged your face so. It was all a terrible mistake."

"I'm glad to know it was a mistake," I said.

She took another drag, reached forward and stubbed it out in the desk ashtray. She hadn't wanted to smoke—just to make the gesture.

"I'm being blackmailed," she told me abruptly. "I thought you were one of the blackmailers."

"And now you think I'm not?"

Gretchen Forrest nodded. "I know you aren't. The man I was expecting did show up. After—you left."

"And did *he* get a dose of the Mungo treatment, too?"

She made a rueful face. "No. You see, I already thought *you* were him. And when *he* showed up right after you'd gone, he took me by surprise. I had to give the money they'd demanded and he was gone before I could do anything about it."

"And how does Mungo enter into it?"

"Al Mungo is a neighbor. We've gotten to know each other pretty well." She grinned a little. "You don't get colorful neighbors like him everywhere. I get a kick out of him."

"Yeah. He's a million laughs, all right."

"You wouldn't guess it about him," Gretchen Forrest said, "but Al Mungo's one of the most overeager social climbers I've ever met. He can't do enough for people he feels are above him. When this blackmailing business started, I couldn't think of anyone else to turn to. I was told that a man I didn't know would come for the money. Mungo told me to phone him when the man came. But *you* came. So naturally I thought you were him. You certainly can't blame me."

"Certainly not," I said.

"When Sam announced you, I phoned Mungo. When you told me who you were and all, I suspected I'd made a mistake. But then you began talking about Sondra Lomax, and that damned party at my place Tuesday night, and I decided you must be that man, after all, just playing it mysterious to confuse me."

"Hold on," I told her. "How did my mentioning Sondra Lomax and your party make me a blackmailer?"

"Because I *knew* Sondra Lomax was one of the blackmailers. And it was at that party that they took that picture of me."

"You'd better start at the beginning," I said. "Because so far I'm way behind you."

"That party," Gretchen Forrest said, "that *was* the beginning. Sondra Lomax was there. And so, apparently, was this man I told you about. There were a lot of people there I didn't know. Anyway, I got plastered pretty early, and I don't remember seeing him. It seems he had a little camera, and he took a picture of me. Then I guess he left, with Sondra. The next afternoon—Wednesday that was—Sondra came to my home again. With the picture. She showed it to me, and demanded ten thousand dollars for all the copies of it and the negative. She said the man who took it would come for the money Thursday night."

"And he did show up, after I did," I said. "And you gave him the money?"

"Yes."

"What did he look like?"

"Oh—tall. Broad shoulders. About forty-five, I'd guess. He had red hair, getting bald. And a mustache." Gretchen Forrest thought for a while, shrugged. "That's about all I can tell you about him."

"And now," I said, "they want more money."

"Yes. How did you know?"

"They usually do."

Gretchen Forrest opened her handbag, took out an opened envelope. "This came in this morning's mail."

The envelope was addressed to Gretchen Forrest with a typewriter. It had been sent airmail special delivery. There was a Las Vegas postmark, dated the day before.

I took a small photograph and a folded sheet of letter paper out of the envelope. Looked first at the picture.

It was a shot of Gretchen Forrest sitting on Larry Score's lap on her living-room sofa. No one else showed in the picture. She had an arm around Score's neck, a liquor glass in one hand, and Score had his hands on her in a way that most people wouldn't have considered correct even in private.

That was it, all of it. They were both fully clothed.

I put the photo down on my desk and looked at Gretchen Forrest. She was gazing fixedly at a spot on the wall behind my head.

"It hardly, I pointed out, "is the sort of picture you'd think would be worth ten thousand bucks' blackmail money."

"You don t understand," she said, not looking at me. "Larry

has a very bad criminal record. And I have a son. Bobby. His father is Vance Stuart. I suppose you know of him."

Uh huh. Vance Stuart was an aging movie star. According to what I remembered from my newspaper reading, he'd been Gretchen's third husband. Or maybe her fourth. She'd divorced him for the usual reason—infidelity—and won the divorce on the usual grounds—mental cruelty."

"Bobby is out on the Coast paying his annual month's visit with Vance. When we were divorced, I had no trouble winning custody of Bobby for eleven months of the year. Vance was playing leapfrog over too many beds to want to be saddled with an infant son. But now Vance is getting old and tired, and Bobby's growing up. Vance sees himself in Bobby. He wants permanent custody of Bobby now. But he *won't* have him. Bobby's mine and I'm going to keep him!"

You see all kinds of greed in my business—for money, for sex, for power. But the look of greed that came over Gretchen Forrest when she spoke of her son was one of the most intense that I'd ever seen. I thought of what a custody battle had done to *her,* and felt a deep pity for the future of that boy.

"Sondra Lomax," she went on, more calmly, "threatened to send this picture to Vance. It doesn't mean anything. I was just drunk and kidding around. But Vance's lawyers would be able to say that a woman who consorted with known criminals was no fit mother for Bobby. I *can't* let that happen. But I don't want to go on being blackmailed, either."

I put the photo down and unfolded the sheet of letter paper. Like the envelope, it was typewritten. No signature. It read: "We forgot to give you all of these. If you want the rest, send the same as before to Jane Smith, care General Delivery, Las Vegas."

I refolded the letter and looked at Gretchen Forrest. "Exactly what do you want me to do?"

"See to it that Sondra stops blackmailing me. And that this picture doesn't get to the papers, where it can harm my chances with Bobby. I worked out a sort of plan on my way here. Couldn't

I send a letter to Jane Smith at Las Vegas General Delivery, but with no money in it? Then if you could hop a plane there, and catch them when they pick up the letter . . . ." She shrugged. "Well, I suppose *you* could find some way to make them stop annoying me."

"Probably," I told her.

"I'll pay you double whatever your usual fee is," she assured me eagerly. "And your expenses, of course. I don't care how much it costs. Just so long as you succeed. I'll pay you a bonus, if you do succeed."

"How much of a bonus do you have in mind, Miss Forrest?"

"I wish you'd call me Gretchen."

I nodded. "The bonus?"

She pursed her lips and gazed at me thoughtfully. "How would three thousand dollars do?"

"It would do rather well," I told her.

I believed I had it figured now. It would explain why I hadn't run into any of Mungo's boys on the way to the office. The session in Captain Jones's office had put a crimp in Mungo's death plans for me. I hadn't been able to back up my claim that he'd been trying to have me killed. But I had made the charge. And if I *was* murdered, it would look bad for Mungo. He'd probably be able to wriggle out, but it would bring unwanted pressure on him. So, if my guess was right Mungo had decided to get me off his back another way. He'd sent Gretchen Forrest to detour me. If I didn't believe her story, I might believe her money. The idea was for me to leave for Las Vegas, and stay there waiting at General Delivery for someone who'd never turn up. With Gretchen paying me double fees and expenses, I shouldn't mind enjoying Las Vegas for a long time. When I got tired of that, I could have her bonus in exchange for going along with the gag.

That was one way to figure this.

But there *was, of* course, always the possibility that Gretchen was telling me the truth. In which case there was no sense in kicking a three-thousand-dollar bonus in the teeth. It didn't necessarily have to detour me. Because whether she was lying or telling the truth still hung on finding the answer to what had happened to Sondra Lomax.

I agreed to take on the job.

Getting out a case sheet, I typed up the bonus agreement. I was to get the three thousand in exchange for making certain that Sondra Lomax ceased to constitute any kind of annoyance or threat to Gretchen Forrest. Margo, from the next-door office of my lawyer, Ben Silver, witnessed our signatures and put her notary public seal on the agreement.

After Margo left, Gretchen Forrest said, "Well, now I suppose I'd best make out a check for you, as a retainer."

"No," I told her. "That won't be necessary. I'll send you a bill."

"But you'll need your plane fare. There'll be expenses."

"Whatever I spend working for you," I assured her, "will be included in my bill."

She didn't know quite what to make of that. She tried to make out something from my expression.

"Well," she said finally, "shall I send the letter now? The one to Jane Smith?"

"Not yet," I told her. "I've got a few other things to clear up first. I'll let you know when to send it."

Her lips tightened. "I don't think I like that. I want you to start on this right away."

"I am. In my own way. And that's the only way I ever handle a case for any client. My own way. If that doesn't suit you, you're free to give the job to somebody else. There's still no obligation between us. You won't have paid me any money, and I won't have done any work."

"But it's *you I* want," she protested. "I—I feel I owe it to you, after what happened to you because of my mistake. And anyway, I *know* you. I feel I can trust you."

"Then do it. Trust me. I'll let you know when to send that letter. If I find it's necessary."

She still didn't like it. But she couldn't think of anything to do about it.

I got up and walked her to the door of my office. After she was gone, I relocked the door, went back to my desk, and phoned a newspaperman I traded favors with from time to time.

It didn't take him long to come back with the information I wanted. It surprised me.

14.

GRETCHEN FORREST *DID* HAVE A SON NAMED BOBBY, according to my friend at the newspaper. Bobby *had* gone out to the West Coast for his annual month's stay with his father, Vance Stuart. And this time Stuart wasn't sending the boy back. His lawyer had filed an appeal to reverse the original custody ruling. Stuart's appeal was scheduled to go to court in Los Angeles the following month.

So Gretchen had told the truth. The question was whether she'd cleverly mixed some truth with a bunch of lies.

I thought it over while I drove my Olds to a repair garage. The garage was only five blocks away but I traveled twelve blocks getting there. If anyone was tailing me, I wasn't able to detect it.

For an extra ten bucks, the garage manager promised to have the replacement for my bullet-damaged windshield in by nine P.M. I caught a cab to the hospital. I wasn't able to spot anyone following me during that ride, either.

A new cop was sitting guard on Gronsky. He used the room phone to check with Santini before allowing me to talk to my client. Gronsky was as I'd left him—lying flat on his back with his shattered leg up in the air.

He greeted me with, "Any luck, pal?"

"Give me time. And the answers to a couple of questions would help."

Gronsky glanced at the cop who sat with his chair tilted back against the wall. "Questions? With him here?"

"Let's try a harmless one, anyway," I said. "Remember the first time we met, you told me you'd seen a guy come out of your girl's place carrying a couple suitcases?"

Gronsky's head nodded on the pillows.

"Was that guy a redhead?"

"I dunno. Had a hat on."

"Did he have a mustache?"

He frowned, concentrating. Then he said, flatly, "No mustache."

"You're sure?"

"No mustache."

"Was he a tall man? Broad-shouldered? In his forties?"

"Naw," Gronsky told me. "He was younger'n that. Kinda short. Built pretty solid, though."

"Fat-solid or hard-solid?"

"Hard."

I felt a tremor of excitement.

I went on to the next question. "Know a guy named Larry Score?"

"Sure. He used to be Sondra's guy, before I come along."

I frowned. "You took Sondra away from Larry Score?"

"Sort of. I knew her from 'way back. I run into her again down here in Miami. So I gave her a play, and she dropped Score."

"Must have made Larry Score kind of angry."

"I guess so. One day I come in and found him with Sondra. Trying to talk her into coming back with him, I guess. I started to toss him out, and the bum pulled a gun on me. So I take the gun away from him. Then he pulls a knife on me."

Gronsky smiled, remembering. "You know what I did?"

"I'm surprised he's still alive," I said.

Gronsky laughed. "Naw. He wasn't that much've a bother. I just took the knife off him and cut his pants off with it. Then I got him over my knee and used his own knife to cut my initials in his rear end."

The cop leaning against the wall said, "The D.A.'ll be glad to hear about that."

"He couldn't prove it," Gronsky said. "Larry Score'll sure never admit it. It'd be bad for his rep."

"A guy like Score," I said, "wouldn't take something like that lying down."

"That yellow bastard? Not him. I told him the next time I caught him bothering Sondra, I'd rip open his ribs and cut my initials on his heart. Any time I ran into him after that, he got out of my way fast."

I digested that for a moment. Then I asked Gronsky, "Can you tell me why Mungo wanted you?"

Gronsky looked at the cop again. "Hey, cop, I got twenty bucks. Wanna take it—and a short walk?"

The cop laughed. "Very funny."

Gronsky looked back at me. "Sorry, pal."

"Does the same go for talking about the boat?"

"Uh huh."

I told him I'd be seeing him, and left.

In the hospital lobby I looked up Danny Yale's home phone number, used the booth to call it. After his phone rang six times, I tried his joint in Miami Beach.

There the phone was picked up on the second ring. A man's voice said, "Frenzy Club." It sounded like the bartender.

"Danny Yale there?"

"Yeah, he's here. You want to—"

I hung up, left the hospital and took a cab across the bay to Miami Beach.

What with Miami Beach's lavish helpings of sun, sin and sand, a tourist is likely to acquire a thirst most any time around the clock. The Frenzy Club was already open for the day, though no brunchtime drinkers had as yet trickled in when I arrived. The chairs were stacked on the tables, the stage was dark and the only one in the place was the bartender, cleaning up behind the bar.

He didn't remember me. He gave me that good old Miami Beach sucker smile and asked, "What's your pleasure, sir?"

"Business. Where's Yale?"

"In his office, doin' the books." He turned his head and yelled toward the rear of the club, "Boss! Guy here to see ya!"

The door beside the stage opened and Yale came out. The gray suit he wore had been cut to order to make his short, stocky figure look taller and slimmer. He hadn't been getting much sun, and the darkness of his slicked-back hair made his tough face look pale.

He remembers me. His mean little eyes squeezed almost shut and he strode across the quiet room to me and snapped, "What the hell do you want? I told you to keep out of my place. Remember?"

I nodded. "Sure I remember. I remember something else you said, too. You claimed Sondra Lomax phoned you on Wednesday and quit to go to Las Vegas with some guy."

Danny Yale eyed me warily for a moment, unsure of what I was getting at. "That's what I said. And that's what she did. So?"

"So how come she didn't pick up her clothes from her apartment?"

"She did."

"No," I said softly. "You did."

If he'd had the sense to bluff it through, I'd have had no way of being certain my hunch was right.

But he didn't. Because he didn't know where I'd got the information, or how lacking in detail it was. He blinked, and stared at me for a few moments. But he was cool enough when he did finally speak.

"I don't know what you're getting at," he said. "Sure I picked up her things for her. All I meant before was that she got them, had 'em with her when she left for Vegas."

"How come you had to get her stuff for her?"

"She asked me to. When she phoned and said she was quitting. She said she had a lot've other things to do, and would I do it for her and leave it for her at the airport baggage counter. So I did."

"You must be a pretty nice boss. A girl quits on you and you go to all that trouble."

"It wasn't much trouble. And she's a good kid. She's pulled a lot of dough into this place for me."

"How'd you know which clothes in that apartment were hers, and which were Maria Barreto's?"

"They used different closets and bureaus," he said slowly. "Sondra just told me which was which. No problem."

"You keep losing girls lately," I said, switching the subject on him abruptly. "First Sondra. Then Maria Barreto."

It didn't throw him. He said, "Yeah." And shook his head sadly. "That poor kid. I'm glad they caught the guy that strangled her. Hope he gets the works for it."

I tried another fast switch. "That party at Gretchen Forrest's Tuesday night. You were there. With Sondra Lomax. Did you see a balding red-haired man with Sondra? Maybe with a camera?"

Danny Yale wiped his hands nervously on his hips. "Redhead? I don't know. There was too many people."

"How about the camera?"

"I don't—" Then he seemed to readjust himself. "Listen," he said, his voice suddenly hard again, "I can't waste time with you. Run along and find somebody else to talk to."

"Who did Sondra leave that party with?" I asked him.

Yale growled, "I guess you don't hear so good. I said I got work to do."

"What *time* did she leave that party?"

Muscles bunched along Danny Yale's jaw. "I told you to get out," he said softly. "I told you nice. But I guess you don't know what nice is."

"I know what an accessory to a murder is," I told him. "And that's the rap you're nailing yourself with if you don't stop lying."

Yale reached his hand across the bar, palm up. "The billy," he said to the bartender. And to me, "Some guys you got to knock things into them before they—"

The bartender had taken a cut-down baseball bat from under the bar. He put it in Yale's open hand.

I sliced Yale's bicep with the stiff edge of my left hand before his fingers could close on it. His knuckles hit the bar and the bat bounced out of his hand and rolled along the bar as his whole arm went dead.

Then I slapped him with my right hand. I slapped him as hard as I could, twisting my whole body into the slap. My palm made a noise like a rifle shot against the side of his face. His head jerked around like it was going to twist off his shoulders. The rest of him spun around after it. He fell down on the bar rail and slumped off it in a half-sitting position on the floor. His hands grabbed at the back of his neck. A sobbing sound of pain came out of him.

The bartender jumped a couple steps along the back of the bar and snatched up the baseball bat. Then he started to come at me.

I looked at him and he stopped coming.

I was mad. Not just sore. Mad. Like Gronsky the Mad Russian was mad. I'd taken it from Mungo and Shev and Frenchy. And then, just when I was beginning to get over it, Yale had tried to give me another dose with a baseball bat.

The bartender looked at my face. He put the bat back down on the bar between us and took his hand off it.

I looked down at Yale. He was still sitting on the floor holding his neck and moaning.

"Cheer up," I said viciously. "I'm going now. Maybe I won't be back. But don't bet on it."

Then I turned around and found myself facing a handsome, blond-haired killer named Larry Score.

He'd come in while I was looking at Yale, and he'd reached the end of the bar. The fury must still have showed in my face. He reacted to it instinctively when I took a step toward him. His hand blurred with motion and came up with a pushbutton knife, the long, wicked blade snicking out of the hilt.

"One more step," Score breathed, "and you're dead. I owe you for sapping me, anyway."

He was poised beautifully on the balls of his feet, his knees slightly bent, his shoulders hunched forward for a thrust. He held the knife expertly, the blade up and out, pointed at my face.

I had instincts of my own. Especially the instinct of self-preservation. I stopped moving toward him.

He was smiling, not at all unsure this time, all of him suddenly as deadly as his eyes.

"Why'n't you go for your gun?" he whispered. "Go ahead. *Try* for it. Give me an excuse. See if you can get it out before I cut your belly open."

I didn't intend to try unless I had to. I wasn't Gronsky.

I edged away from the bar, watching him tensely. "You'd be making a mistake," I said. "Some customers are likely to come walking in here any second. Mungo wouldn't like your doing it in his club, either."

I saw it register. He didn't lunge at me with the knife. But he didn't let me increase the distance between us, either. He moved as I did, not letting me get far enough away to draw my gun before he could get the knife into me. I drifted in the direction of the club entrance, watching him every step, making a wide berth around him, my hand poised to go for my .38. Score turned slowly, facing me, the blade of his knife moving in a short menacing arc, the point slicing the air between us, back and forth. It was like two fighting cocks circling warily, each waiting for the other to make the first move.

I reached the door.

"Another time, Rome," Larry Score promised in a whisper.

I backed out of the Frenzy Club.

On the pavement, in the bright sunlight filling Collins Avenue, I almost bumped into a man and woman in bathing suits. The man grinned and said, "Drunk so early? And we thought *we* were rushing it." The woman with him laughed. They went into the Frenzy Club. I turned and walked away, fast.

And kept walking, for ten blocks, till some of the pressure pent up inside me began to ease.

One thing was certain. If Mungo *had* sent Gretchen Forrest to me to get me off his back, he'd soon hear that it hadn't worked.

Which meant that his death sentence was once again walking at my heels.

15.

I'D HAD LUNCH, AND TWO SNIFTERS OF BRANDY to relax me enough to digest it, when I took a cab out to Hialeah. It was a perfect day. A cloudless sky, a cooling breeze, the grandstands and clubhouse packed with spectators, the swaying palms and fluttering flags— all adding up to a carnival atmosphere.

Most real gamblers won't go near a track. The long wait between each race makes the betting action too slow. They prefer the fast turnover of dice, blackjack or roulette—or the fierce, unremitting struggle of poker. When they feel like playing the ponies, they place their bets through their bookies. But I'd never failed to get a special excitement out of watching the jockeys in their bright colors pounding their thoroughbreds around a hard, fast track with every ounce of speed that had been bred into them.

I was there for another reason that day. But even so, as I entered the clubhouse, I caught some of the infectious spirit of the mob, which already had their money riding their hunches.

The third race was running when I arrived. I worked my way through the yelling crowd in the clubhouse stands, searching for Kit Forrest. I finally spotted her down at the bottom row of seats. Going down the aisle till I reached her row, I stood there watching her root her bet around the track.

It struck me that each time I saw Kit Forrest, she was different.

The first time, at her home, she'd looked self-assured, almost fiercely independent. The second time, when I'd watched her through the binoculars, she'd seemed a solitary, lonely figure. Now she was different again.

She wasn't sitting in her chair. She stood with her hands gripping the rail, her figure rigid with tension, her face shining with a reckless excitement as she yelled at the horses tearing up the turf around the last turn.

As the jockeys flogged their mounts across the finish line and the results went up on the tote board, she let go of the rail, made a rueful face. She tore up her bet stubs, let them flutter through her fingers.

I moved over beside her and said hello.

She turned her grave eyes on me. Then she remembered, and smiled. "Oh! It's you. My fellow long-shot plunger."

Her smile did to me what it had done the last time. She looked vibrantly lovely in a pale-blue dress. The sun caught highlights like dark flames in her roan hair.

"What in the world happened to your face?" she asked.

"I ran into a couple guys."

"Looks more like they ran into you. I suppose that happens, if you're a private detective. You see? I remembered about that. But I'm sorry—I've forgotten your name."

"Rome. Anthony Rome."

"I *am* poor about names," she apologized. "But I won't forget again. Promise. How've *you* made out so far today?"

"I just got here," I told her. I gestured at the scattering of torn-up tickets at her feet. "Tough luck."

"Oh, I didn't really expect to win. I've been playing the longest long shot in each race."

"You could try running your money through a meat grinder to see if it came out rubies instead. The odds would be better."

"I know. All too well. But it's the only way I can work up a lather about a race. I lose so often that when one of them starts to look like a winner, even for just a couple seconds, I feel like

Columbus discovering America."

"You do have a problem," I said, straight-faced.

"Don't mock me, sir. Wait till *you* have more money than you can possibly use. Then you'll see how hard you have to work at having fun."

"I'm likely to be spared that," I said. "What about that little sailboat of yours? Have to work at enjoying that?"

She looked at me thoughtfully, shook her head. "No. Sailing is different. I've been doing it since I was a kid. Whenever it gets so that I can't stand people around me, I go out on the water and pretend I'm the only one in the world. It works."

"I know. I've got a boat, too."

"What kind?"

I told her about the *Straight Pass.*

"You must do very well at the detective business," she said.

"I won the boat in a crap game."

She laughed and patted my chest with a slim hand. "I think you're going to grow on me, Mr. Rome." She glanced out at the tote board, took up her tip sheet from her chair. "Now let's see which horse is supposed to come in last in the next race."

I'd picked up a racing form before taking the cab to the track, and spent the ride studying it. "Let's bet Fancy That. He's a long shot for you. And he's got a chance."

"Fancy That?" Kit Forrest looked at the board. The odds for my hunch were fourteen to one. She looked up the statistics on Fancy That in her sheet. "Sounds just right for me," she announced. "He hasn't won a race in two seasons."

"But if you'll notice, he has a habit of finishing stronger than he starts. And he's always been in six-furlong races up till now. This is his first go at one-and-sixteenth miles. He's got more time to stage his finish sprint."

Kit Forrest went over the figures again. "You're *right.* It sounds reasonable."

"A gambler with a hunch can always think up a reason for it."

"How true. Well, shall we?"

We did. She accompanied me to the five-dollar window while I bought three tickets. Then I went with her to the hundred-dollar window. She bought one ticket.

By the time they froze the betting before the start of the fourth race, the odds on Fancy That were down to eleven to one. Which meant some other people were playing the same hunch.

Kit Forrest hadn't been exaggerating what betting a long shot could do to her. As we waited for the starting gun, she watched the track with fierce concentration. I absorbed some of her fever. When the horses broke out of the gate in a tight tangle and Fancy That took an early lead, we both jumped to our feet. Kit gripped my arm as though she were trying to break bones.

Two lengths later, our horse suddenly went into slow motion. Four other horses swept past him as though his feet were in molasses. For most of the rest of the race, Fancy That was lost to sight in a cluster of dawdlers trailing the favorite and a contender.

But as they came around the last turn, my long shot shook off his lethargy. He suddenly broke out of the pack, gathered up a head of steam and came tearing up the track after the two front-runners.

Beside me, Kit Forrest began pounding the rail with her fists and screaming, "Come on! Come on! Come *on!*"

I was yelling myself.

Fancy That, heady with his newly acquired jet propulsion, caught the front-runners two lengths from the finish line. And charged across, winner by a neck.

Kit Forrest threw her arms around me. I put my hands on her slim shoulders and resisted the impulse to make more of it.

"Well," she breathed, sagging with release of tension as she let go of me, "fancy *that!*"

We grinned at each other like kids as we headed back to the windows to collect our loot. My hundred and sixty-five dollars; her cool eleven hundred.

"Come on," she said eagerly, "let's pick the next race while we're still hot."

We lost most of what we'd won on the remaining races. But

she didn't lose the triumph she'd gotten from that fourth race. By the end of the last race, there was a comradeship between us that it would have taken me weeks to achieve any other way.

As we worked our way among the mob surging through the parking area, I suggested having dinner at the Chesapeake House, if she didn't have a date.

"No date," she said. "Not till later tonight."

We climbed into her white Jaguar. I said, "What time's your date? We wouldn't want to keep Paul Mungo waiting."

She looked at me oddly. "What makes you think my date's with Paul? It isn't."

"I'd heard you and Paul Mungo were considering marriage."

"Whoever told you that?"

"Al Mungo."

Kit shook her head and grinned crookedly. "He's just indulging in wishful thinking. Mr. Mungo is embarrassingly eager to belong to what he considers high society. I suppose he feels if I married his son it would automatically gain him entrance to the ranks of the exalted. Meaning people like me and Gretchen. It's pathetic, a man like him thinking there's still such a thing as class."

"Then it's not true? About you and Paul Mungo?"

"Not a chance."

"Odd. Mungo acted so certain that there was something between you and his son."

Kit gripped the wheel of the Jaguar and frowned. "I'm afraid he's been misled. And it's partly my fault. Paul has some girl he's afraid his father wouldn't approve of. Funny, isn't it? Mungo being the strait-laced parent? But he is. So sometimes when Paul goes out with her, he tells his father he's got a date with me. He got me to agree to back him up on it. Appealed to the romantic in me. But if Al Mungo is starting to think of himself as my future father-in-law, it's time to call it quits."

She maneuvered the Jaguar out of the parking area and headed for the Chesapeake House. She drove the way she played the horses. I had my feet pressed hard against the floorboards and my teeth grinding together most of the way.

At the Chesapeake House we took a secluded booth in one of the little rooms with dim lighting that somehow managed the effect of being under the cool sea. The atmosphere was enhanced by the seashell-covered walls and all the derelicts dangling from the ceiling—models of sailing ships, colored bottles, ancient ships' figureheads, stuffed fish of all kinds.

As we finished off the steamed clams and started on the lobster, Kit said, "You know, this place is one of the few things I really like about Miami."

"Not a bad town. It has its points."

"For you, maybe. You live here, work here. But for a tourist like me . . . ." She shook her head. "The mixture of a frantic, New York-type pace with the seashore calm irritates me. I like places to be one way or the other."

"So why come here?"

"Gretchen likes it. And she begged me to come with her. She can't stand going anywhere alone."

"She's not much like you, then," I said. "Every time I've seen you, you've been alone."

"I don't know too many men around here," Kit explained. "The few I do know—well, it would be bound to end up with my having to squirm out of an entanglement."

"Why squirm out?"

"I've witnessed too many object lessons in entanglements. So no, thanks. I'd rather stay free."

"Gretchen," I said, "just picks the wrong kind of men."

"That's a fact," Kit admitted. "She has a penchant for dangerous husbands and boyfriends. Dangerous for her nervous system."

"Especially her latest," I said casually.

"Larry Score's not so bad. At least he acts as though he likes her. That's more than a lot of her men have. I'm afraid Gretchen has a big streak of the masochist in her."

I chewed some delicious-looking lobster without tasting it.

"You've got one strong attachment, it seems."

"To whom?"

"Your sister."

Kit nodded slowly. "After Father died, our aunt and uncle won custody of us. They were cold potatoes with no real love for children. The only warmth I had, as a kid, was with Gretchen. She seemed like more of a mother to me than a sister, even though she was just a child herself."

Kit suddenly grinned. "I guess I just love her, and that's it."

I let the conversation drift.

Over our after-dinner brandies, Kit said, "By the way, the date I have later tonight is at Reggie's. Why don't you come along? We were lucky together once today. Maybe it'll happen again."

"Your date might not like my joining the party."

She shrugged. "It wouldn't be much of a loss if he didn't. How about it?"

I shook my head. "Got a busy night ahead of me. Work."

"Oh? What are you working at? Anything interesting?"

"Routine. I'm trying to locate someone."

"You make it sound dull."

"A lot of my job is."

"I'll bet it's not really. Judging from those bruises on your face. If you want to know what dull really is, try living the life of the idle rich for a while."

"It can't be all dull," I said. "I hear that was quite a shindig your sister threw at your house last Tuesday night."

Kit frowned, thinking back. "Oh, I remember. It was a wild one, all right."

"Were you there through all of it?"

"God, no. It was still going on when I came home late that night. Early Wednesday morning, actually. They were whooping it up. Without Gretchen, by then. I guess she'd already passed out. Anyway, I just went up to my room and went to sleep."

"Notice Al Mungo around when you came in?"

"No, I didn't see him."

"How about Larry Score and Danny Yale?"

"They weren't there, either. They usually *are,* at Gretchen's parties. So I guess they'd already gone home." Kit suddenly looked at me with narrowed eyes. "Hey! You're pumping me, aren't you?"

I smiled. "Just a little."

"*That's* why you came over to me at the track. To wheedle information out of me."

"Partly."

"Very sneaky, Mr. Rome. Now I don't feel bad about forgetting your name." But her grin took the sting out of it. 'Why don't you try just asking me right out whatever you want to know?"

"Okay. I'm trying to find a girl who used to work at the Frenzy Club. Sondra Lomax. I asked you about her before. You said you didn't know her."

"I still don't. The Frenzy Club. Al Mungo owns that place, doesn't he?"

I nodded. "It would help me if I could find out when Sondra left that party. And whether she left with anybody. I asked your sister. She didn't know."

"Gretchen didn't remember anything about that party the next morning. She must have *really* hung one on."

"Nobody I've met so far seems to remember much about that party," I murmured.

"Why are you trying to locate this girl?"

"Because she's hard to locate. It would help if you could put me next to some of the people you saw at that party."

"I don't know many of Gretchen's friends. We don't . . . ." Kit hesitated, thoughtful. "Wait. There *was* one man there I do know. Arnie Sherwin."

"Who is he?"

"An artist. Of sorts. He makes money sketching caricatures of people in nightclubs and at private parties. He has a knack of making his caricatures both funny and flattering. So of course he's quite popular. I've seen him keep a party amused for hours, doing caricatures of each of the guests. For a fat fee from the host."

"Where do I find him?"

"I'm not sure, at the moment. Want me to try finding him for you?" '

"I'd appreciate it."

"I'll ask around," Kit said coolly, "*if* you tell me what this is all about."

"I did tell you. Sondra Lomax used to work at the Frenzy Club. She isn't there anymore. Every time I try to find out where she's gone, I run into something like this." I touched the tender place under my eye.

"I have a sudden thought about Arnie," Kit said. "I've seen him sketching people at Reggie's a couple times. So why don't you come along? He might be there tonight."

I considered it, shook my head. "I can't spare the time tonight, if he isn't there." I got a pen from inside my jacket, wrote my office phone number on a napkin and pushed it to Kit. "Will you phone me if Arnie Sherwin *is* at Reggie's tonight? Or if you find out where he is? I won't be at this number, but you can leave a message."

She took the napkin. "And you claimed your job was dull. I suddenly feel like the Marines coming to the rescue."

"You just hold onto that feeling," I told her.

***

The way I spent the next six hours after parting with Kit Forrest would have disillusioned her. It was the plodding part of my job.

First I got a small copy of Sondra Lomax's photograph from Headquarters. I took it to the airport and showed it to the man behind the baggage-checking counter. He couldn't recall if a woman looking like her had picked up a couple suitcases Wednesday or Thursday. That didn't necessarily mean that she hadn't. He just didn't remember her. And he kept no permanent records by which he could have determined whether Danny Yale really had left the suitcases there to be picked up by a Sondra Lomax.

I moved around the terminal and showed the picture to everyone who worked there. No one remembered her.

Nor was there any Sondra Lomax listed on any of the flight records going anywhere out of Miami the past Wednesday, Thursday or Friday. Not that that proved anything, either. She could have used a false name, posing as the wife of the balding red-haired man.

If there actually was such a man.

It was ten o'clock at night when I finished drawing my blank at the airport. I put through a call to my office. An answering service took all my calls there after five P.M. They had no message for me from Kit Forrest. I took a cab to the garage where I'd left my car to have the new windshield put in.

Picking up my Olds, I drove to the railroad station to try my photo of Sondra Lomax on the people working there. Then I tried the bus stations, and a number of the largest car-rental companies.

Nothing.

It was two in the morning when I called my answering service again. There was a message for me this time, but not from Kit.

It was from Danny Yale.

I put through a call to the Frenzy Club. When I got Yale on the phone, I said, "This is Rome. You wanted me to call you."

"Yeah," he said through the phone. "I been waiting." He sounded nervous. "Listen, Rome. I been thinking over what you said. About me being accessory to a murder. I don't know about any murder. That I swear. But the way you were talking, there's some kind've trouble going on. And that's something I can do without. Come over here now, and I'll tell you anything I can."

I didn't say anything for a couple heartbeats. He'd talked too much and too fast. I hadn't said anything to scare him that much. "I'd prefer meeting you at the Middy," I told him. That was a bar across from the Dade County Courthouse. As safe a place as I could think of.

"I can't make it there," Yale told me angrily. "The club don't close till five in the morning and I never get out till six. You want to talk to me about something, you come here. Otherwise, forget it."

I hadn't the faintest hope that Danny Yale was really prepared to open up. But if he was willing to talk—even double-talk—there was always the chance I could push him into saying something interesting.

I thought about the Frenzy Club. It would be packed at that hour. And the street outside would be full of lights and people.

It wouldn't be easy for Mungo's boys to get at me with all those people around. If I used elementary caution, they wouldn't be able to get at me at all.

"I'll be right over," I told Yale, and hung up.

16.

I DROVE SLOWLY ALONG COLLINS PAST THE FRENZY CLUB. I didn't
see anything that spelled danger. The street in front of the club was
all lit up. Enough people were still strolling and driving along
Collins. On the wide veranda of the hotel across the street from the
club, two couples were engaged in a game of cards. I circled the
block and cruised past the club again. Then I corkscrewed the Olds
into a tight space at the curb of a side street two blocks away.

Before getting out, I reached under the dashboard and got the
little gun I kept taped there. It was a .22 repeater automatic, with
six shots in its self-ejecting clip. I stuffed it up into the left-hand
sleeve of my jacket. It just fitted. One hard shake of my arm would
drop it into my hand. I took the .38 Special out of my belt holster
and put it in the right-hand pocket of my jacket, leaving my hand
in the pocket with it. Two-gun Anthony Rome.

The sports-jacketed, cigar-chewing puller at the club entrance
grinned as I hesitated there.

"Plenty of time to see 'em all take it off inside, mister," he
coaxed cheerfully. "Continuous show. No cover or minimum at the
bar. Lotsa girls to pick from. They're takin' it off right now."

He held the door open and I went in, my right hand gripping
the metal in my pocket. I halted just inside, studying the place
carefully. Up on the stage a long-haired blonde in black-lace bra

and panties was doing the changing-for-bedtime act. There was a bed on the stage, and the blonde stood before a big oval mirror, swinging her hips to the band music while she pretended to powder her arms with a huge powder puff. Then she stripped off the black-lace bra and began powdering her big, high-set breasts with the puff. The mirror had no glass in it, and it faced out to the audience.

There was a lot of audience. The tables were all taken, and the bar was crowded. None of the B-girls latched onto me this time. They were busy working all the men already there.

At my end of the bar a curvy brunette drinking with a florid-faced man who was playing the loaded big shot suddenly asked him, "Honey, mind if I have wine this time?"

The florid man, assuming she meant an ordinary glass of wine, grinned and caressed her bare shoulder and said, "Sure, kid. Why not?"

I felt sorry for him.

The brunette told the bartender to bring the wine. He did. A big bottle of champagne. The florid man stared, dumfounded. The brunette helped to keep him off balance by picking up his hand and kissing the inside of his palm. "Golly," she murmured to the sucker, "I feel so passionate tonight. You must think I'm terribly bold."

The sucker continued to stare in sick fascination at the bartender working the cork out of the bottle, his mouth moving as he tried to get up the nerve to protest. Then the cork popped, and it was too late. The bartender set two champagne glasses on the bar with a flourish, poured them full.

"That'll be thirty dollars for the bottle of wine," the bartender told the man pleasantly. "No offense, sir, but we have to collect as we serve, when it's a whole bottle."

The sucker, his face more florid than before, got out his wallet with trembling fingers, pulled out a ten, three fives and five ones. There wasn't much left in the wallet when he stuck it back in his pocket. The brunette picked up her glass of champagne and said, "Well, here's to fun, lover."

The sucker nodded dazedly, picked up his glass. He choked down some of the champagne as though it were lye.

I let my glance slide the length of the bar, taking in each man there. Then I surveyed the rest of the room again.

Nobody seemed to be paying any attention to me. I started toward the door beside the stage. The bartender glanced my way. His mouth opened in surprise as he recognized me. I wondered about that. I'd have expected him to know I was coming, so he could tip Yale when I arrived.

I opened the door beside the stage and went into a short, narrow corridor. There was a curtained doorway to the girls' dressing room, and a closed door. The forefinger of my right hand touched the trigger of the .38 in my pocket. I held my left arm ready to shake the tiny automatic out of my sleeve. I didn't feel in the least bit silly about all the artillery.

Turning the knob of the closed door, I pushed it open—hard—so it swung all the way and banged the wall. Just to make sure nobody was waiting behind it. Danny Yale sat behind the desk of his office. There was a chair on my side of the desk, a file cabinet and a studio couch. There were no windows in his office. But there was a door behind Yale, probably leading to the back alley behind the club.

I stood where I was for a few seconds, making certain there was no one else in the office. Then I stepped inside, shut the door, and leaned my shoulders against it while I watched Yale and the door behind him.

Yale folded his hands together on top of his desk and said, "You made it fast, Rome. You must be pretty anxious."

"You had something to tell me. Tell it."

He shook his head. "No. I said if you had some questions, I was ready to answer the ones I can." His tough, pale face was tight. "If there's something going on I don't know about, I don't wanta get caught in any bind. I don't know about any murder, but—"

"Yes you do," I told him. "There's Maria Barreto, for one."

"*That* what you meant? Hell, they got the guy did that."

"No. Gronsky didn't kill her. You know that."

"I don't know anything of the kind. If it's Maria's murder you were talking about, I got no worry."

"There's Sondra Lomax, too."

"She went to Las Vegas."

"I don't think so. I think she was dropped in the ocean with her feet stuck in a block of cement. After she'd been knifed."

Yale shook his head. "Couldn't've been her. Sondra phoned me Wednesday and—"

"Isn't it possible," I suggested, giving him enough rope to hang himself with, "that it wasn't Sondra who called you? It could have been another woman, imitating Sondra's voice."

Yale frowned. "It's possible, I guess. It sounded like Sondra, but—"

"But you didn't actually see Sondra on Wednesday, did you?"

"No. That's so. I ain't seen her at all, since—"

He didn't finish it, so I finished it for him: "Since that party at Gretchen Forrest's on Tuesday night."

Yale nodded slowly. "Yeah." He appeared to consider it. No one tried to open the door I leaned against. The door behind Yale stayed shut. Just the two of us in that room, having a quiet talk. No danger at all, on the surface. I didn't like it.

"Tell me about that party," I said.

"Nothing special to tell," Yale said. "Just a big party with a lot of laughs."

"How did it start?"

"The way those things usually do. Larry Score and Gretchen Forrest came into the club a little before midnight. I joined 'em. Business was slow right then, so Sondra sat down with us. Then Larry says, why'n't we all go to Gretchen's and drink in comfort. So we did, the four of us. We got to feeling good, and decided to make it a big blast. Larry and me went out to get more people. We split up and each of us went hunting for the right kind of people, and we brought 'em all back to Gretchen's and threw a big one. Real good night it was, too. Everybody high, but no fights. Just a ball."

"Was Gretchen's kid sister there?"

"Uh uh. She ain't like Gretchen. She's kinda square, some ways."

"What time did the party break up?"

"I dunno. I latched onto some doll and cut out around three in the morning."

"I thought Sondra Lomax was your date?"

"Yeah, but when I looked around for her she wasn't there. I guess she cut out earlier with some other guy." Yale grinned and shrugged. "You know how broads are when they get loaded."

"Who did she leave with?"

"I told you, I didn't see her go. Maybe this guy she went to Vegas with."

"She didn't go to Vegas."

"So you say, Rome. But I don't hear anything to prove she didn't. What the hell, if this is all you got, why're you trying to scare me?"

I probed at him a while longer, but he didn't change his story, and I didn't get any more out of him.

Finally I said, "Why did you call me to come here? This is just a waste of time."

"Not my fault, Rome. You're the one thought we had something worth talking about. So goodbye."

"This," I warned Yale, "was your last chance to get out from under."

He grinned. "Under *what?*"

I got hold of the doorknob behind me with my left hand. Then I yanked the door open and leaped aside.

There was no one in the corridor, and Yale didn't take his hands off the top of his desk.

Yale laughed. "Pretty jumpy, ain't you."

I slammed his office door shut and made my way out of the Frenzy Club as slowly and cautiously as I'd come in. Outside, the doorman grinned at me. "What'sa matter, mister? Broke already?"

There were plenty of people along Collins, but none that I knew. The card game was still going on across the street. I walked away from the club. At the end of the block I turned around suddenly. No one was following me.

When I reached the side street, I stopped and studied it carefully before approaching my car. No one was waiting for me at the Olds. I got the flashlight from the glove compartment, opened the hood and looked inside. Then I squatted down and flashed the light under the car. Nobody had rigged dynamite to the starter or the wheels. I opened the car trunk. No one was hiding in it.

Getting behind the wheel of the Olds, I got the flask from the glove compartment, took a deep swig of brandy. I kept the brandy in my mouth, tasting it, before swallowing. No one had put anything in it.

I drove away, circling several blocks. No car tailed me. I stopped at an all-night sundries store and used the phone booth to call my answering service. No message from Kit.

It was three in the morning by then, and I was beginning to run down. I wasn't going to go back to my boat. Mungo was certain to have some of his killers staked out there by night. So I chose one of the big hotels lining Miami Beach along the sea, had the hotel garage attendant take my car and checked into a room under a false name for the night.

I awoke in the morning to find myself charged with the murder of Danny Yale.

17.

IT CAME OVER THE RADIO IN MY HOTEL ROOM while I was shaving with a razor I'd had a bellboy bring up. I had the bathroom door wide open and the radio turned up so I could hear the morning news. I heard it loud and clear.

Danny Yale, manager of Miami Beach's popular Frenzy Club, had been bludgeoned to death in his office last night by one Anthony Rome, a former Miami police lieutenant now working as a private detective. I had caved in Danny Yale's skull with a tire iron.

I put the razor down on the sink. In the bathroom mirror, I saw blood where I'd dug the blade into my cheek. I went into the bedroom and stood there staring at the radio, listening to the rest of it.

According to the police, the commissioner reported, I'd had an argument and a fight with Danny Yale earlier yesterday in the Frenzy Club. The bartender who'd witnessed it said I looked furious when I stalked out.

Then, late last night, I'd come back into the club, and walked straight through to Yale's office. I was in the office with Yale for about ten minutes. Then I came out and left the club.

The bartender, worried because he remembered my fight with Yale earlier that day, hurried back to the office to make sure Yale was all right. He wasn't. He was slumped over his desk with his head bashed in. The tire iron that killed him lay on the floor.

The police figured that I had carried the tire iron under the jacket of my suit when I entered the club. I probably hadn't taken it back out with me because of all the blood on it. They figured I'd panicked after killing Yale, dropped the iron and left in a hurry. There were no fingerprints on the iron—so either I'd covered my hand with something before swinging it on Yale or I'd wiped the prints off afterward.

The police had no doubts about me being the killer. Yale had phoned them, about five minutes before I'd entered the Frenzy Club last night, and said he was afraid I was out to kill him. He told the cops over the phone that I'd just phoned him, sounding drunk, and unjustly blamed him for a beating I'd taken earlier in that week. I'd threatened to kill him for it. Yale had demanded that the cops protect him. He hadn't realized I was going to make good my threat so quickly.

I'd disappeared after leaving the Frenzy Club. I hadn't returned to Dinner Key, where I lived aboard a boat. All the police in Miami and Miami Beach were hunting for me. Headquarters asked everyone to be on the lookout for me and report immediately if they saw me.

The commentator read off a disturbingly accurate description of me and of the clothes I'd been wearing last night—the only clothes I had with me in the hotel room. He said that my picture— filed with the police department when I'd renewed my investigator's license that year—was being shown over television. He described my car and gave its license number.

I switched off the radio and stood there, a queasy feeling in the pit of my stomach.

Yale had been persuaded by someone to ask me to visit him at the club last night. And he'd been persuaded to make the call to the police, claiming I'd threatened his life over the phone, while I was on my way there. He'd been talked into believing it was part of a plot to put me out of action. It had worked, too. But Yale certainly hadn't realized that his death was part of the plot to nail me.

I *was* nailed. The murder frame was too tight for any lawyer to get me off.

My only chance was to pin the kill on the real murderer before I was caught. I didn't think much of my chance of staying free long enough to accomplish that. Not with my picture in the papers and on television. Not with half the cops in the area knowing me personally, and the rest carrying copies of my picture. The only reason the cops hadn't come for me yet was that I'd used a false name on the register.

If the room clerk who'd signed me in, or the bellboy who'd brought up the razor, saw my picture over TV, this hotel was a trap. If the hotel garage attendant had heard the radio broadcast describing my car, he'd check my license plate, then make a fast call for the cops.

I unfroze fast. Wiped my face with a towel. Stuffed my red tie in the pocket of my blue suit jacket and wrapped the jacket around my holstered gun in a tight bundle. Carrying it under my arm, I opened the hall door.

The garage attendant was getting out of the elevator down the corridor, walking toward me. He was a burly, muscular young man. Which was probably why he'd been picked to keep tabs on me till the phoned-for cops arrived.

So I had maybe two minutes, at the most, to get out of the hotel.

The garage attendant stopped uncertainly when he saw me.

"Ah—mister—" he mumbled. "Your car—got a flat tire. I just come up to tell you."

"Fix it for me, will you?" I said, closing the distance between us.

"You'd better come down and have a look at it first," he said, gaining confidence.

"Later," I snapped, and started past him.

He didn't have any weapon, but he had guts. He made a grab for me. I twisted on my heel and jabbed my bunched, stiff-held fingers into his solar plexus. His eyes glazed and his knees buckled and he bent down. I hit him carefully behind the ear with the edge of my hand, caught him as he fell and eased his unconscious form to the floor. Then I hurried the length of the hall, past the elevator doors, opened the fire-exit door and started running down the stairs.

At the bottom I opened the metal door and stepped out into a wide service alley between my hotel and the next one. As the metal door shut behind me, locking itself, two Miami Beach prowl cars whipped past the front end of the alley and screeched to a halt at the hotel entrance.

I sprinted the other way along the service alley. Forcing myself to slow to a walk as I went around the rear of the hotel, I hurried through a palm-shaded courtyard and out into the blazing sunlight of the cabana-surrounded hotel swimming-pool terrace. About a dozen early risers were already sprawled on beach mats around the pool, getting their vacation money's worth of morning tan. Some of them eyed the way I was dressed as I skirted the pool and went down three tile steps to the beach.

The wide strip of golden sand stretched away on either side of me between the endless row of hotels and the gentle surf of the ocean. There was no one else using the beach yet that morning. Far out at sea several charter fishing boats were heading across the Gulf Stream, rocking like tiny white chips on the heavy swells. Farther out, a freighter moved along the horizon, steaming south.

I longed to be on any of those vessels, going anywhere. On that long strip of empty beach I stood out like a wart on a movie queen's nose. I turned right and began running along the beach, kicking up fountains of dry sand that got into my shoes.

My chances of getting away had been slim before. Now they were so thin as to be almost nonexistent. The cops knew where I was. And Miami Beach was one of the simplest places in the world to seal off. It is a long, slender island, with only four causeway bridges connecting it to the mainland across Biscayne Bay, plus a short bridge at the northern Bal Harbour end of the island.

By now the news of my whereabouts had been radioed in. All the bridges would be blocked off, each vehicle crossing them stopped and searched. A huge police dragnet would be closing in on this immediate section of Miami Beach. As for the water— every police boat and available Coast Guard cruiser would be starting the job of circling the island, with lookouts searching through binoculars. They'd close in on anybody swimming from Miami Beach out to sea or across the bay; they'd stop and search any boat leaving Miami Beach in any direction. And they'd be aided by a couple seaplanes and helicopters.

It was like being corked in a bottle. No building or street was safe. It wasn't just the cops I had to worry about. In a couple hours everybody on Miami Beach would know about it and be on the lookout.

The last desperate hope left for me was to find some way to keep on the move through Miami Beach the rest of that day, to elude the searching dragnet till night. In the darkness, I might be able to escape by water.

I ran, floundering in the soft, deep sand, past about four hotels. I still wasn't close to where I was headed, but I couldn't chance staying exposed on that empty beach any longer. The cops who'd zeroed in on my hotel would be spilling out behind it to the beach any second.

So I turned and left the beach, forcing myself to a walk as I entered the pool terrace behind a tall pink-and-white hotel. I kept going, straight through the hotel and out its glittering front lobby to Collins Avenue. I headed south along the pavement, toward Lincoln Road, which is Miami Beach's plush shopping street. I could count on its being crowded at that time of morning.

I'd covered a couple blocks when I spotted a patrol car turning the corner a block ahead. I turned off the pavement, not hurrying, into the hotel I happened to be passing at the time. Inside the lobby, I strolled to the newsstand and bought a paper. There was a card with sunglasses mounted on it on the counter. I bought a pair. The news dealer hardly looked at me as he gave me change. He was concentrating on a racing form.

I stuck the paper under my arm with the jacket wrapped around my holstered gun. As I crossed the lobby, I put on the sunglasses. They didn't do much in the way of changing my looks, but it was a start.

The patrol car had gone past by the time I emerged.

I'd made another block when I saw a patrolman trudging toward me down the same side of the street, looking straight ahead in my direction. I was in luck. I didn't know him. If he'd been one of the dozens of cops who knew me personally from my police days, he'd have recognized me even at that distance. As it was, I couldn't let this one have a closer look. He kept coming, glancing into each hotel he passed. I turned casually into the next hotel I came to.

A bellhop confronted me as I stepped into the lobby. "Got your luggage waiting outside, sir?"

"I just came in after a pack of cigarettes," I told him, cringing inwardly as he looked me full in the face.

He jerked a thumb over his shoulder. "Machine over there."

I went past him on slightly shaky legs, crossed the lobby to the cigarette machine. I took my time putting in the coins and getting my pack of Luckies. I drifted sideways behind a potted palm. Took more time opening the pack, knocking out a cigarette, lighting a match.

The patrolman appeared in the lobby entrance, glanced around inside. I raised my hands to my face and lit the cigarette. He turned away and walked on up Collins.

I knew this wouldn't last much longer. As soon as they pulled enough cops into the area, they wouldn't be satisfied with mere glances. Cops would start filtering through every building, combing every floor. And my walking into any lobby would become more and more dangerous as the news about me and my description spread. Every hotel employee would be on the lookout for me. So would the tourists drifting in and out; they'd be getting a little extra excitement bonus with their hard-earned vacations.

I dropped the cigarette and stepped on it, left the hotel and continued down Collins toward Lincoln, watching out for cops every step of the way.

Lincoln Road was, as I'd expected, crowded with shoppers sightseeing the luxurious window displays. I merged into the crowds surging along the sidewalk under the vivid, multicolored store awnings. I turned into the first drugstore I came to, bought a waterproof plastic bag big enough to hold my .38.

The next place I entered was a sports store. I bought a towel and a sailor hat, wrapped them in the jacket under my arm. Then I went out and merged with the Lincoln Road crowd again. I walked quickly, knowing my time for this sort of thing was running out. The police would expect me to do exactly what I was doing— getting myself a change of clothing. They'd soon start combing the stores.

Two blocks farther on, I turned into a men's clothing shop. I went to the back, where the beach clothes were. I purchased a pair of red beach sandals, green-and-orange-checked Bermuda shorts and a flowered sports shirt. When the clerk turned his back on me to ring up the purchase and get my change, I snatched a pair of plain, dark-blue swimming trunks from the counter bin marked with my size. By the time the clerk turned back to face me again, I had the swimming trunks out of sight inside my rolled jacket.

I used the store's dressing room to change. Shucking out of my shoes, socks and clothing, I pulled on the dark-blue swimming trunks. Then I put the checked Bermuda shorts on over that and got into the flowered sports shirt and the red sandals. I stuck my gun and money in the plastic bag, except for some change, which I put in the pocket of my swim trunks under the shorts. Zippering the plastic bag shut and folding the flap down over the zipper to make sure no water could get into it, I stuck the package it made under the waistband of my shorts. With the bottom of my sports shirt hanging outside the shorts, the bulge was hidden. I stuck in the sailor hat, too, wrapped the towel around my waist.

Everything else I had I wrapped with my suit and shirt and

carried back out to the clerk, to be wrapped. The clerk blinked at the sight of me in the red sandals, checked shorts and flowered shirt. But he managed to hold back his laughter. He'd have no trouble remembering that gaudy getup when the cops came in asking after me. He'd be able to describe exactly what I'd been wearing.

I left carrying the clothes he'd had wrapped in a package for me, and hurried back along Lincoln to hotel row on Collins. My vividly clashing outfit created no interest. There were plenty of others around.

As I reached the junction of Lincoln and Collins, two cops came out of a hotel to my right. I knew one of them.

Before he could get a look at my face, I turned left into Collins Avenue and strode away from them. I wasn't recognizable from the rear. Not in that getup. Not yet.

But there was a police car parked in front of a hotel a couple blocks ahead of me on Collins. The dragnet was growing, tightening.

I turned off the pavement and walked around the side of a sprawling, two-story motel. Reaching the pool area in the back, I entered the rear of the motel and called over the first bellhop I spotted. I gave him my wrapped package, tipped him two quarters to check it under the name William Jonas. He assumed quite naturally that I was a patron of the motel who'd made some purchases and was too lazy to carry the package up to my room before going out again.

Going back out to the rear of the motel, I cut over through a grove of palms and subtropical hedges to the hotel next to it. I went into the hotel through the side bathers' entrance. The room corridor inside was empty. Working fast, before anyone came into the corridor and saw what I was doing, I shucked out of the red sandals, the checked shorts and the flowered shirt. There was an incinerator slot in the wall. Opening its metal hinge-door, I tossed sandals, shorts and shirt down the slide, to be burned in the incinerator.

Then I unwrapped the towel from around my waist and put on the sailor hat, pulling down the brim. It would hide my hair and give my forehead and the sides of my face a little concealment. I wrapped the plastic bag containing my gun and most of my cash inside the towel and walked out to the hotel pool wearing only the blue swim trunks, sunglasses and sailor hat.

That area was still too dangerous for me. The greatest concentration of searching cops would be there, where I'd last been seen. I had to work my way out.

I didn't attract any attention as I skirted the pool area this time. I was dressed for it, just one of the many tourists sunning and swimming. I went out onto the beach. There were some people out on the sand by then. But still not enough. When I spotted two cops coming out of a hotel onto the beach up ahead of me, I looked at the ocean.

There was already a police patrol boat there, about five hundred yards out, cruising very slowly parallel to the shore.

I hesitated, glancing back to the pool terrace I'd just left. There were plenty of people there. But it was too dangerous in this area. They knew I was somewhere around here. The cops would be checking every possible concealment, taking a careful look at every single man.

I headed into the ocean surf.

When I was out chest-high, being smacked by the waves, I held my hands underwater, got the plastic package out of the towel and stuck it with my sailor hat and sunglasses in the tight elastic waistband of my swim trunks. Then I tied the soaked towel around my waist and started swimming.

I swam out from the beach. Far enough out so the cops prowling the length of the beach wouldn't notice my head sticking out of the water. Not far enough out to attract the interest of the patrol boat. Then I turned and began swimming north, parallel to the beach and its endless row of gleaming-white hotels.

From the water, that row of waterfront hotels really did look endless. Miami Beach has over four hundred hotels and motels packing its slender length, and a surprising percentage of them manage to squeeze into that line along the ocean. I swam past six of them, side-stroking leisurely. I was in no hurry. I still had most of that whole damn day ahead of me.

I cut in toward shore as I passed the sixth hotel. I had a long way to go before getting out of the worst danger area. But I couldn't take the whole distance in one swim. The lookout on the patrol boat would spot me and start wondering why I was swimming that far. Most swimmers stick close to the short chunk of beach belonging to their hotels. And if my actions made the lookout curious, the patrol boat would whip over and haul me aboard to satisfy that curiosity.

As I got near enough to the beach to stand up, I took the plastic package and my sailor hat from my trunks, wrapped them in the wet towel, put on the sunglasses. Then I waded out onto the dry sand. There still weren't many people on the beach; nor were there likely to be too many more even by mid-afternoon. I silently cursed the tourists who paid extra for a beachfront hotel, then stuck to the swimming-pool terraces.

I walked the beach past three more hotels, then went up onto one of those pool terraces. A hotel pool boy headed my way almost the second I appeared. You can always tell a pool boy by that look of eager, cheerful cunning. He was carrying a pencil and a clipboard.

I forestalled any questions by speaking to him first as he reached me. The pool boys watch out for interlopers from other, less desirable hotels.

"You the pool boy?" I asked him.

"Yes, sir. Are—"

"I got this towel wet," I said. "I was so anxious to get in that ocean, I went and took the towel in with me. I'd like a dry one."

"Surely, sir. This is your first day, right?"

"That's right."

He poised the pencil over the sheet on the clipboard.

"Your name?"

"Harold Barnes."

He wrote it down. "Room?"

If I gave him a room number that he already had down for another name, he'd get suspicious. I gave him a silly grin. "This is foolish of me, but I've forgotten it. I just got here, you see, and I was in such a hurry to get in for my first dip that—"

He smiled with benign understanding. "I know how it is, sir. I'll get your room number from the desk later, and charge everything to it. You'll be wanting a mat, won't you?"

I said I would, because he'd have wondered if I hadn't.

"I'll get it for you," he said. "Along with that dry towel. Want me to take the wet one?"

"No," I said. "It belongs to me personally."

That puzzled him a little. But he went away and came back with a dry towel and a red-and-green-striped beach mat. He laid it out for me next to the pool. As I stretched out, he squatted down beside me and said softly, as though he were launching a conspiracy, "Anything you want, sir, I'm the boy to get it for you. That means *anything*. Like say introductions to some girls, you know?"

"That's nice to know," I murmured, wishing to hell he'd go away and stop studying my face so thoroughly. I knew that he was only watching for my reaction to his between-the-lines suggestion, but he wasn't going to have any trouble remembering what I looked like when he saw my picture in the papers or on TV. Or in a cop's hand.

If he hadn't, already.

"Now you take that girl across the pool there. The redhead?"

I looked across the pool. A deliciously curvy young thing in a very meager two-piece swimsuit was flaunting her figure and flaming red hair at about seven guys of all ages who were keeping her company.

"Those guys don't mean any real competition," the pool boy assured me confidentially. "She still ain't met any guy here that she goes for. And she's got another week to go. So—well, you can't lose anything trying, anyway. You never know, sir, you might be the one she's been waiting for."

"I think I'll just spend today getting the sun."

"You got a pretty good suntan already," he observed, wondering about it.

I didn't want him to wonder. About anything. "I've been down in South America on business. Rio. Pretty good sun there, too."

"Yeah? I heard Rio's a real hot town." He winked. "But take it from me, there's no place you can have more kinds of fun than right here in Miami Beach."

A very pale man and woman came out of the hotel and saved me. The pool boy murmured, "Remember, see me if you get interested in anything." He jumped up and went over to greet them.

I lay face down on the mat and tried to relax a bit. The sun warmed into me, and the soothing sound of the surf reached me, and the sensual laughter of the red-haired girl drifted across the pool. But I stayed tense.

I was thinking that it was time to head back into the ocean when a uniformed cop came out of the hotel onto the terrace. My mouth went dry.

He looked around the terrace, slowly, carefully. I put my face down on my folded arms and listened to my heart thudding against the tile of the terrace. Out of the corner of one eye, I saw the cop look at me, keep looking at me a few seconds, then look away. That didn't mean that it was all over. He'd just begun to check the place. Next he would do it in detail, place by place, person by person.

He started with the places—the cabanas. He went to the first cabana, knocked on the closed door. No answer. He tried the knob. It was locked. The cop called over the pool boy, started to talk to him.

They had their backs to me. When the cop reached into his shirt pocket, my heart stopped. I knew what he was reaching for. He was getting out a photo of me to show the pool boy.

18.

I GOT OFF THE MAT AND OUT OF THE POOL-TERRACE AREA as fast as I could without running. I reached the beach, out of sight, before they turned to look where I'd been.

Moments later, when the cop hurried down from the terrace to the beach, followed by the pool boy, I was out in the ocean, clutching my plastic bag in one hand and the sunglasses and sailor hat in the other. The instant I saw them appear, I sucked in a deep breath and went underwater.

I stayed submerged as long as I could. Longer than I'd have thought I could. When I came up, gasping for air, the cop and the pool boy were out of sight.

For once I was grateful that not many people used the beach. No one had noticed me going into the ocean, or the cop would still be on the beach, trying to signal the patrol boat while he sent the pool boy in to make a call to headquarters.

As it was, the cop couldn't be sure it was really me the pool boy thought he'd seen. From past experience, I was willing to bet that at least one-third of the people to whom he'd already shown my picture had thought they'd seen somebody like me.

But I didn't take any chances. Stuffing the plastic package, hat and sunglasses under the band of my trunks, I started swimming north parallel to the beach once more.

Praying that the cop didn't know that I was out there. Because if he did, there'd be cops waiting in hiding for me anyplace I went ashore.

I swam past about a dozen hotels this time. Keeping watch on the patrol boat out there and the shore as I cut through the dips and hills of salty water. Each time I put a couple hotels behind me, I dove under the surface, swimming submerged till my lungs demanded more air. Each time I came up, I changed my swimming style—from side stroke to crawl to breaststroke to floating on my back and propelling myself by scissoring my legs. Then back to side stroke. Unless the lookout on the patrol boat started watching me steadily through his binoculars, he wouldn't realize I was the same swimmer making all that distance. There were others in the water. From four hundred yards away one swimmer's head looked pretty much like another's.

But that kind of trickery could go on only so long before the lookout got wise. So after putting the dozen or so hotels behind me, I steeled myself to take the chance I had to take. I swam toward the beach.

I selected a place where there were five or six people sunning themselves on the sand. I trudged out of the surf slowly, eyeing the palm-dotted pool area behind the hotel. Nobody grabbed me as I came out of the water. This time I didn't go up to the pool. I sat down in the sand, waiting. No cops appeared.

Finally I stretched out on the beach, trying to take advantage of the brief rest. I was breathing hard and my arms and legs felt weary—more from tension than the swim. I began to breath more easily when I saw the patrol boat out there pick up speed and diminish to the north. When it was almost out of sight, I went back into the ocean, resumed my long swim.

I swam slowly but without interruption this time, sticking to a steady crawl. I put another fifteen hotels behind me before I glanced back and saw another police boat slicing up from the south in my direction. I cut into the beach again, sat on the sand till I saw two uniformed cops appear several hotels away. They trudged along the beach toward me, stopping to talk to every person they came to. I got up and strolled off the beach into a palm-shaded little park behind two hotels. I went through the rear of one hotel, crossed the long, wide patio of another where men and women in bathing suits sat at wrought-iron tables drinking and having lunch. I remembered that I hadn't had anything at all to eat yet that day.

Cutting down toward the beach again, I came to a long row of beachside cabanas, sporting red, yellow and green awnings and facing out to sea. I slipped into the narrow space between two of the cabanas and peeked out at the beach. The two cops had just gone past, were working their way slowly along the sand toward the south, stopping at each beach lounger they came across.

Ducking back between the two cabanas, I put on my sunglasses, squeezed out the sailor hat as much as I could and stuck it on my head. I got a five-dollar bill out of my waterproof bag, folded it in my hand, and went on north between the beach and the hotels toward the one where the cops had first appeared.

There weren't likely to be more cops there, for a while at least. And it was one of the largest hotels in the area. Which meant there would be a lot of people out behind it.

By the time I reached my objective, the hot sun was drying my hat. And I found the crowds I'd expected. Between the big hotel and the beach was a vast area of sprawling terraces, vivid-colored tent cabanas, awnings and lofty royal palms, all centering around an enormous swimming pool some fifty by ninety feet, shaped like the top of a grand piano. Near it was a small, circular children's pool.

The little pool was packed with squealing, splashing kids, being supervised by a hotel lifeguard while their parents relaxed on beach mats. In contrast, there were only a few swimmers in the huge, sun-drenched adult pool. But there were plenty of people using the terraces surrounding it—sunning themselves on lounging chairs on the open terraces, eating, drinking and playing cards at bright red-and-blue tables on the shaded ones.

I sat down at one of the few empty tables on a stretch of lawn shaded by palm trees and huge pink umbrellas. Almost instantly a white-jacketed waiter appeared with a menu. I had a look at the prices and settled for a club sandwich and a glass of brandy—which, with the tip, cost me the entire five dollars.

I was ravenous and thirsty, but I forced myself to eat slowly and sip the brandy. There was a certain feeling of protective coloring from the other people dining around me and the ones playing gin rummy at a couple of the tables. Most of them were wearing only bathing suits, though none of them looked like they'd been near the water as yet that day.

I didn't let the brief sense of safety among numbers lull me too much. I kept an eye on the approaches to the terrace, ready to run at the first sign of a police uniform or any guy who looked like a plain-clothes cop. And when I suddenly realized that three girls in bikinis at the table next to mine had stopped chattering among themselves and were staring at me, I experienced a stomach flutter that interfered with my swallowing.

It came to me that the bruise under my eye was still discolored and that part of the bruise probably showed despite my sunglasses. The description of me that had been broadcast had included the fact that my face was bruised.

I lowered my sandwich and looked at the three girls. All three of them gave me coy-bold smiles. I began to feel better. I even smiled back at them.

One of them said, "You're just new here, aren't you? We haven't seen *you* before."

Back home up North, probably, none of them would ever make a pass. But they were eager for the fun they'd come far and paid hard to get. And the girls outnumbered the men in Miami Beach. Unless a girl was very pretty indeed, she had to work at cornering her share of male companionship.

I said gently, "Why, yes. My wife and I just arrived an hour ago, as a matter of fact. She was tired from the trip. She's taking a short nap in our room."

It was as though I'd turned off a switch. They stopped smiling at me and went back to chattering among themselves. I went back to my lunch.

A formal announcement came over the loudspeaker hung from one of the palm trees. "Attention, please! Attention, please!"

I tensed.

The voice over the loudspeaker went on, in the same tone of quiet urgency. "Two canasta players are needed *immediately.* Repeat: *Two* canasta players are needed immediately. Apply at the front desk. Thank you."

I relaxed and finished my sandwich. As I swallowed the last of the brandy, I was feeling better. No hunger. No one chasing me for the moment. I began to consider staying right there for a while as I ordered cigarettes.

The waiter brought the pack of Luckies, opened it for me with a flourish as though it were an operation requiring superb skill. He even popped one cigarette out for me.

I didn't want to delve in the plastic bag in front of him. So I paid him from the change in the pocket of my swim trunks, tipping him a quarter.

He stood there and gave me a freezing stare as I lit the cigarette. He was used to bigger tips from the clientele of this hotel. And the employees in Miami Beach establishments are experts at making cheapskates squirm.

But then the quality of his stare changed subtly. It ceased being merely intimidating. He began really to look at me.

I became very conscious of the bruise under my eye. It seemed to grow.

He turned and walked off. I watched the way he did it. Before, he'd wandered among the tables, watching eagle-eyed for the chance to perform any tip-worthy service. Like retrieving a gin-rummy card that had fallen off a table. For a dollar. But this time he strode straight away from my table into the hotel.

I took a deep drag at my cigarette, dropped it in the table ashtray and left the terrace. Zigzagging my way among the other terraces, I crossed the beach and went back into the ocean.

For the rest of the afternoon I continued swimming gradually northward, resting briefly on the beach and swimming north again. It worked fine.

Until about five o'clock.

Then people began disappearing from the ocean, the beach and the pools, going into their hotels to get ready for dinner. All except the cops. They didn't disappear.

By six o'clock, I was one of the few people left out in the open anywhere between the hotels and the ocean. Soon I'd be the only one. With a couple more hours of daylight left to go.

I couldn't use the streets or hotels. Not wearing only swimming trunks, at that time of evening.

I was swimming, trying to figure out what I was going to do, when a Coast Guard launch hove into view. It was cruising south, about three hundred yards out. As it came even with me, it slowed down. By then, I was the only swimmer in the ocean.

I made a fast turn and swam in to the beach behind a massive, modernistic hotel. I crossed the empty strip of sand, strode through the deserted pool terraces.

Inside one of the hotel's bathing entrances, I found what I was hunting—a public phone booth. I needed Jack McComb now. If I could manage to stay free till night, and McComb could bring his boat offshore so I could swim out to it.

I dropped in the coin and dialed the number of the phone booth on our pier down at Dinner Key. A man answered it. I recognized his voice. He kept a small houseboat moored at our pier.

Altering my voice, I asked, "Is Jack McComb around?"

"No. He took a party out early this morning. They headed down to the Keys for a few days' fishing."

So that was it. No help from McComb. And he'd been the only one I could be sure would be willing to help me at the risk of getting himself nailed for aiding a wanted murderer. I hung up and stood in the booth searching for another way out. There *was* one other way. Risky as hell. But I couldn't come up with anything safer.

19.

WHEN I CAME OUT OF THE BATHERS' ENTRANCE, the hotel pool boy was dumping disinfectant into the swimming pool. He was the only one around, and he was about my size. So he would have to do.

He looked up at me with quick interest as I approached the pool. "Hi, there. Figuring on a last dip?" I nodded.

"That was the idea."

"Not in here," he warned. "That stuff I just dumped in'll burn your eyes like fire when it's concentrated. Got to wait a couple hours before it thins out through the whole pool."

I shrugged. "No dip, then. Oh, well . . . ."

"You're new here, aren't you?" he asked politely, and we went through the whole business of my having just arrived, and having acquired my tan while down in South America on business.

"Got a cigarette?" I asked. "I don't feel like going back up to my room for one yet."

He said, "Sure," and led me to his cabana, which was a combination office, first-aid station and place for storing towels, beach mats and terrace umbrellas. It was small, windowless. He got a pack of cigarettes from his locker. Lit one for me. Then he launched into his spiel about being able to furnish me with anything I wanted during my stay in Miami Beach.

"Like say you rent a car while you're here. You got to pay by the mile, right? So why pay it all? Just bring the car around to me. I know how to fix the speedometer. That way you can ride it around all you want, and when you take it back it only shows maybe ten, fifteen miles you got to pay for."

"Clever," I said.

He shrugged modestly. "I figure, what the hell. I save a nice guy like you some dough that way, you'll probably pay me for my trouble, out've what I saved you. Right?"

"Stands to reason."

"Got a date for tonight yet?" he asked.

"No."

"I'm your boy in that line, too," he assured me. "Just tell me what you've got in mind. If you like the amateurs, there's plenty of free stuff down here on vacation I can put you next to. If you like more excitement, I know some gals that'll give you a hot time for the right price."

"I'll keep that in mind," I told him. "But tonight all I want is a lot of sleep."

"Okay. Just remember, when you're ready . . . ." He glanced at his watch. "I've got to change now and sign off the job. Got a date tonight."

"Just a minute," I said. I opened the plastic bag and took out the gun and showed it to him.

He gaped at it as though he couldn't figure out what it was. But he stood perfectly still and didn't make a sound.

"It's this way," I told him quietly. "I need the suit you've got hanging in that locker there. And I need this cabana till dark."

He found his tongue. "*You're* that guy they've been looking all over for!" he whispered shakily. *"That's* who you are. The killer."

"Right," I told him. "Don't make me kill you, too."

"You *crazy?"* he blurted. "Why should I make trouble? I didn't know that guy you killed. So what do I care? You want my suit? *Take* it. You wanna stay here? Go ahead."

"It's not that simple, unfortunately. There's always the chance you might decide to get brave."

"Me? Not me."

"You *know* I can't take the chance," I said regretfully, and hefted the .38 in my hand.

"Please, mister!" he squeaked. *"Don't* slug me with that thing."

"You'll have to co-operate, then."

He co-operated. He sat in a straight-backed wooden chair, holding still while I used surgical tape from his desk to secure his wrists behind him and bind his ankles to the legs of the chair. I got a flashlight from his locker, shut the cabana door and locked it. Then I sat on his desk, keeping the beam of the flashlight on him. I offered him a cigarette, but he shook his head. I took his wristwatch and looked at it. Then I settled down for a two-hour wait.

Half an hour passed, and then someone tried the cabana door, found it locked. There was a knock on the door.

A man's voice called, "Lennie? You in there?"

"That's Mr. Bell, my boss," the pool boy whispered.

"Shut up," I whispered back.

"Lennie!" his boss shouted. "Where are you?" Then, "Damn that kid! Leaving without—" He was walking away, and whatever else he muttered I didn't hear.

I lit another cigarette and settled down to more waiting. The flashlight beam was weak and flickering when I finally opened the cabana door. Night had come. The lights of the hotel shone on the water of the swimming pool. I didn't like the lights. But Miami Beach was as dark as it was ever going to get.

I put on the pool boy's clothes, pulling his trousers on over my damp swimming trunks. His shirt and sports jacket were a little tight across the shoulders, but it wasn't anything noticeable. His shoes were very tight. I put on his straw hat. It was a little small, but I jammed it on.

Putting the .38 back in the plastic bag with the money, I took out three twenties and a ten, dropped them on his lap to pay for the clothes. Then I gagged him with tape, stuck the plastic bag in the jacket pocket and went out.

***

Two dodged prowl cars later, I was across Miami Beach, in a dark, quiet residential oasis lining the bay shore. I slipped across the lawn between two Norman-style mansions, reached the water's edge. Far across Biscayne Bay the lights of Miami gleamed against a dark-velvet sky. There were boats in the bay, some anchored, some moving. Two of the moving ones were police patrols—one far off to my right, the other to my left in the middle of the bay. They were zigzagging, their powerful searchlights swinging back and forth over the rippled surface of the water.

I went into the shallows under the empty wooden dock belonging to one of the mansions. I was weary to my bones. But I had another long swim ahead.

I stripped down to my trunks, stuck the plastic package under the waistband. Kneeling, I pushed the discarded clothing underwater, weighting it down with stones from the bottom. Then I ducked out from under the dock and began the swim.

About two hundred feet out from the bay shore, I turned and began swimming south. I stuck to the breast stroke, smooth and slow, careful to make no splashing sounds with my arms or legs.

I'd been swimming that way for about fifteen minutes when one of the patrol boats began slicing in my direction, its searchlight dancing ahead of it. I looked around quickly, spotted a dark, anchored cabin cruiser. Began churning toward it. The patrol boat was making better time than I could. The distance between us began to close. The dazzling beam of its spotlight stabbed across the bay surface, reaching for me.

I took a deep breath and dove toward the cabin cruiser. I managed to reach it before the air in my lungs gave out. Ducking under the keel, I surfaced on the other side. The sound of the patrol boat engines drew closer. Catching the anchor line, I held my face against the hull with just my nose and eyes out of the water.

The tire fenders of the patrol boat bumped gently against the other side of the cabin cruiser. I heard two of the cops climbing from their vessel to the empty one. I held myself still. Through the hull I could hear their footsteps as they searched.

Then they were going back aboard their boat. I heard its engines rev louder. The patrol boat swung around the cabin cruiser, its spotlight probing toward me.

I ducked down into the water, dragging myself toward the bottom along the anchor line. I stayed down as long as I could. When I came back up to the surface, the police were a hundred feet away, heading toward the shore.

I began swimming south again.

An hour later, I was nearing the island where Mungo and the Forrest sisters had their homes.

I summoned a last burst of speed from the depths of my exhaustion. As I drew close, I saw that the big cruiser at Mungo's dock had lights showing from the portholes of its lower cabin. I angled toward the Forrest villa. I was in luck. The little catboat wasn't at the dock. Which meant that Kit Forrest was probably out for a sail—and would be back before too long.

And Kit was the only hope left to me.

If I could count on her. If she didn't start yelling for the cops the second she saw me. Because by now she must have heard about my being wanted for murder.

I used up the last of my strength reaching the Forrest boat dock. The only light showing came from the inside of the villa, downstairs. I climbed up onto the dock. I was dangerously lightheaded and as limp as though my bones had turned to rubber. The night breeze felt cold against my wet skin, but there was nothing to do but wait and hope.

I must have sat there for almost an hour. I felt numb, heavy-bodied and drowsy when suddenly I spotted her sail moving through the darkness toward me. A second later, a patrol boat swung around and came speeding across the bay after her.

I got up then. Hurried off the dock into a grove of tropical bushes and palms. The patrol boat hove to off the island as Kit tied up her catboat at the dock. Its searchlight caught her. She was wearing a pair of white shorts and a white pullover sweater. She stood up on the pier, one hand shielding her eyes from the glare of the searchlight. I got down on my knees, peering through the bushes.

"Miss Forrest," one of the cops called, "you see anything of a man swimming in the bay while you were out?"

"At this hour?"

"That killer is still loose."

"You haven't caught him *yet?* Not very efficient of you."

They didn't like that. You could hear the cop straining to stay polite as he called, "You see any stranger wandering around, phone it in right away."

"He wouldn't be around here. Your police were all over this island earlier today,"

"Well—he's *somewhere.* " The searchlight left Kit and played over the area behind the house. I ducked lower as it swept the bushes. The searchlight moved on, dipped into her catboat to make sure no one was there. Then the patrol boat swung away and headed off across the bay again.

When it was gone, Kit turned around and called softly,

"Where are you?"

I stood up, emerged from the bushes. Kit, her figure shadowy in the darkness, walked slowly off the dock toward me.

"How'd you know I was here?" I asked her.

"You left wet footprints on the dock." She stopped, facing me, studying me as well as she could through the shadows. "I've been hanging around here all day on the chance you'd phone or something."

I stared at her. "Why?"

"I had a hunch you might not have anybody else to turn to. But now that you're actually here, cold reality is suddenly making me feel very silly. Scared, too, I guess."

"Why did you want to help me?"

"The romantic in me. Didn't you know? In my own way I'm

as idiotically sentimental as Gretchen. I used to daydream about a Prince Charming, like all little girls. Only with me, of course, the story had to be reversed. Because I knew I'd never get a chance to be one of the deserving underprivileged. So it had to be Prince Charming who'd be in trouble, and I'd rescue *him*. An evil moneylender would be foreclosing the mortgage on the old castle and kicking the prince out of the kingdom. I'd come along disguised in rags. The prince would think I was a beggar girl, but he'd fall in love with me anyway. And then I'd reveal myself, pay off the mortgage, buy back his kingdom for him. And we'd live happily ever after."

She was right about being scared. It was making her talk too much, too fast.

I said, "Well, Prince Charming thanks you."

"You," she told me nervously, "were not what I had in mind for the prince. . . *Did* you murder that man?"

"No."

"Of course you'd say that," she said, neither accepting nor rejecting my claim.

She was balanced precariously on the edge, ready to go either way. I tried to think of what to say to her. But my brain was sluggish. I wiped my hands over my eyes, leaned back against the trunk of a palm.

She asked quickly, softly, "What's the matter with you?"

"Nothing." I heard the weariness dragging at my voice. "I've been on the run all day. I've had it."

Kit glanced toward her villa. "We'd better get you inside," she said slowly. She'd made her decision.

"Anybody else home?" I asked her.

"Just Sam. He was in the pantry polishing silverware when I went for my sail. He'll be at it for another hour or so, and at midnight he leaves for home. You'll be safe in my room. Gretchen's out. She probably won't get back till very late."

I let her lead me to a side door of the villa. We went into a small marble foyer and up a flight of mosaic-tile stairs to her bedroom. She closed the door behind us, switched on the light. It was a large, octagonal room, with a bathroom and deep dressing alcove. Unlike what I'd seen of the downstairs, the furnishings here were modern almost severe. Color had been used to soften the effect. Cool blue-green predominated. The brocade-padded headboard of the outsized oval bed had a control panel for the massive hi-fi set centered in one wall, surrounded by shelves of records. Two of the eight walls were taken up by multi-door closets and built-in drawers. Two of the walls were draped, floor-to-ceiling windows looking out on the water. Another wall contained a marble-tile fireplace.

Kit said, "Don't worry about Sam hearing you in here. This is all soundproofed. You could play records full volume and it wouldn't carry beyond these walls."

I trudged to her bed and sat on it, oblivious to what my damp swim trunks did to it. I rested my forearms on my thighs and looked at her, feeling some of the day-long tension leak out of me.

She gazed back at me, her lower lip caught between her teeth. Then her teeth let go of the lip, and she said, "I was thinking. I could rent a cabin cruiser and get you away. Across to Cuba, maybe."

"That's not the kind of help I need," I told her. "The problem isn't how to get away. It's how to stick around and get myself out from under a murder frame."

She smiled for the first time. It was a faint smile, but it was there. "I was hoping you'd say that," she whispered. "What do you want of me?"

"I could use something to eat. And some clothes I can go out in. But the food first. And some brandy. I'm chilled."

"And frightened?"

"Of course I'm frightened," I snapped. "Do you think I'm stupid?"

She shook her head. "No. You're not that. Or they'd have caught you."

She put her hand on the doorknob. Then she thought of

155

something. "I located Arnie Sherwin for you. But I don't suppose you're still interested in—"

"The artist who was at that party Tuesday night? Where is he?"

"He lives over a place called the Cold Eye, in Miami. I don't know the address, but—"

"I know it," I told her. The Cold Eye was a beer joint hangout for self-styled beatniks. "I'll get to him later."

"The police," she reminded me, "are patrolling the bay. And checking everyone using the causeways."

"I'll work something out."

She looked at me for a moment. "I guess you will," she said finally, and left her bedroom, closing the door softly behind her.

She returned carrying a tray with a plate heaped with cold chicken, a bottle of French brandy and a glass.

"I told Sam I wanted a bedtime snack," Kit said as she set the tray on the bed.

The brandy formed a warm core, chasing the chill from my bones. I told Kit what I wanted as I gnawed a chicken leg. There was a shop still open on Miami Beach where she could pick up the clothes. The other item I wanted could be gotten from a drugstore.

Kit stared at me. "Sounds like you're trying to make yourself as conspicuous as possible. Is that wise?"

I nodded. "Best form of camouflage. After you get these things, drive that white Jaguar of yours over to Miami." I told her where to leave it. "Take a cab back here."

She considered me for a moment. "I could get in a lot of trouble, helping you this way. Couldn't I?"

"Nothing you couldn't buy your way out of," I told her.

She looked a bit chagrined. "You take my help pretty much for granted."

I put down the chicken leg and controlled a gust of anger.

"You're helping to save me from spending the rest of my life in prison. Do I have to make a speech for you to understand how grateful I am? You decided to help me. I didn't pressure you into it. If you want to change your mind . . . ."

"No. Calm down." She smiled suddenly. "You have a very bad temper, Mr. Rome."

I surprised myself by smiling back. "So does any cornered rat."

After she'd gone, I wolfed down chicken till I felt full, drank another glass of brandy. It was very good brandy. I was wrapped in a pleasant lethargy as I stripped off my swim trunks and went into the bathroom to get the bay silt off me.

The bathroom was an enormous cave of pink marble. The bathtub alone—sunk Roman-fashion below the level of the floor—was the size of an ordinary bathroom. I climbed down into it, fiddled with the gold-plated handles till I found the ones that worked the shower. Warm water fine-sprayed all over me from the mouths of five gold turtles' heads projecting from the wall on two sides of the tub. I turned the water to hot, then worked it back through warm to cold. I was relaxed and drowsy by the time I climbed out and toweled myself dry.

Tying a towel around my hips sarong-style, I wandered back into the bedroom, drank some more from the brandy snifter. I stretched out on my back on the big oval bed. My eyelids became heavy and closed. I felt myself beginning to float.

I didn't fight it. I knew I couldn't dodge the law much longer. I had a lot to do in the short space of limited freedom left to me. But I couldn't do anything until Kit returned.

And, for the moment, it was an overwhelming relief to know that there was nothing I could do for myself.

Nothing but sleep.

20.

I WAS AWAKENED BY THE WEIGHT OF SOMEONE depressing the mattress. I opened my eyes and looked up at Kit Forrest. She sat beside me on the bed, looking down at me with an expression of grave bemusement.

I asked her, "What time is it?"

"Half-past twelve." She touched a finger to a livid bruise that still showed on my chest. "Did Mungo do that?"

"With a little help." I reached up and lazily ran the edge of my thumb along the firm line of her jaw. Shadows moved in the green depths of her eyes. "Your butler go home?"

She nodded. "We have the place to ourselves."

I sat up. The weariness was gone. "Did you get all of it?

She gestured at a shopping bag on the carpet.

I got off the bed, picked up my swimming trunks and carried them into the bathroom. When I came out wearing the trunks, Kit was standing beside the bed, waiting.

I picked up the plastic package containing my gun and cash, and the shopping bag she'd brought. "How are your nerves?" I asked her.

"All right. So far."

"Hold onto them," I told her. "We're going for a sail."

While Kit raised the sail of her catboat, I stood on the dock estimating the distance of the nearest police patrol boat. It was off to our right, cruising along the bay shore of Miami Beach.

Kit settled in the stern and took the tiller. I cast off the mooring line and climbed down with the shopping bag and plastic package into the catboat, gave it a shove away from the dock. A strong breeze caught the sail and filled it, taking us out into the bay. Kit, handling the boat with expert ease, headed toward the Bay Point shore of northeast Miami. I sat hunched over in the bottom, looking back past Kit toward the ever-present patrol boat.

We hadn't gotten far before I saw it suddenly swing around and come speeding after us.

"They're coming," I told Kit quietly, and got ready to jump.

She nodded, her lips pressed tightly together. She went on sailing as though unaware of anything else.

I waited till I saw that the patrol boat would come up to starboard. Then I went over the port side. I went under up to my nose, held my head against the side of the catboat with my hands braced under the keel. Moments later, the spotlight stabbed out across the catboat, over my head. The police boat slowed, cruised along by the other side of the catboat, keeping pace with it.

"Oh, it's you again, Miss Forrest," a familiar voice said. It was the same cop who'd spoken to her before.

"Yes," Kit answered, sounding utterly untroubled. "Such a perfect wind for sailing tonight. We haven't had many like this. Don't tell me you're *still* looking for that poor man?"

"That *poor man*" the cop growled, "is a killer. And it's not such a good idea, you being out at night like this with him still somewhere around."

"Then why don't you catch him?" Kit demanded haughtily.

The cop made a sound that could have been repressed anger or just clearing his throat.

"Don't worry about me," Kit said. "I'm only going to take one more turn around the water. And if I see anybody swimming, I'll scream so loud all of Biscayne Bay will hear me."

"You do that," the cop snapped.

The engines of the patrol boat revved up. I ducked my head underwater and counted to sixty. When I came up for air, the patrol boat had its stern to us and was cruising toward Miami Beach.

Kit let out her breath as I climbed back into her boat. "How did I do?"

"Magnificent. You should take up acting."

"I did. I was lousy." She swung the tiller and pointed the boat toward Miami.

Fifteen minutes later, we were climbing onto the concrete dike along a short stretch of unlighted waterfront. I put down my packages and looked at her. "You'd better go back now. Before the boys in that patrol boat get suspicious."

"Suppose you need me later?" she asked.

"I'll give you a call."

"I have my own phone in my bedroom." She gave me the number. "If I don't answer right away, let it ring. I may be asleep. And I sleep like the dead."

"Like a girl who's done her good deed for the day," I told her softly.

"Take care of yourself," she whispered. She stood there close to me, looking up into my face and not moving.

I took her shoulders in my hands and drew her to me.

"Tough Mr. Rome," she murmured huskily.

Her lips were firm and full under mine, like ripe fruit. Her body forced itself tightly against mine and her arms went around me. Her lips moved and she gave me a taste of the tip of her darting tongue. Her kiss took on a startling savagery and cunning.

"That," she whispered, pulling away from me, "was for luck." I watched her climb into her boat. She cast off and took the tiller and sailed out across the dark water of the bay. She didn't look back.

In the darkness of an alley between two commercial waterfront buildings, I stripped off my trunks, dried myself quickly with a towel from the shopping bag. Then I got into the clothes she'd purchased for me. Shoes and socks, light-blue suit and a sports shirt. I took the black eye patch from the bag and strapped it on, felt around the edges of it with my fingers. The black leather covered the bruise around my eye completely. I stuffed my cash in my pocket and hung the holstered .38 on the belt under the jacket.

Kit's Mark IX Jaguar was waiting a block away. The ignition key was under the seat. The engine started with a throbbing roar. I snapped on the headlights and drove away into the heart of Miami.

The open white sports car and the black eye patch combined to insure that I would attract attention. I couldn't have been better disguised in a false beard and Halloween costume. No cop glancing my way would connect me with a wanted man who should be doing everything possible to avoid notice.

Unless I did something that caused him to take a closer, longer look at me.

Unless he was one of the cops who knew me.

Unless . . . .

21

THE COLD EYE WAS A FORMER DELICATESSEN, flanked by a secondhand clothing shop and a Cuban diner, both closed for the night. A big white eye was painted on its blacked-out store window. The eye was crying. Its tears were icicles. Somebody inside was doing some angry shouting.

I crossed the street and went into a narrow doorway between the Cold Eye and the Cuban diner. There was a narrow flight of worn stairs going up between dirty walls whose ancient paint was peeling off in flakes the size of my hands. At the top was a single wooden door. The name ARNIE SHERWIN was scrawled on it in red paint. I knocked on the wooden panel. I waited awhile, then knocked again, louder.

After a couple seconds, a sliver of yellow light appeared under the door. The lock was turned, the door swung open. The man who opened it was wearing wrinkled underwear shorts and a sleep-blurred face.

He was tall and fat. His body was hairless and his skull was shaved. A defiant brown beard stuck out from under his chin, but the rest of his face was clean-shaven. He clung to the doorknob with one hand, leaned against the wall with the other and slitted his eyes at me, stifling a yawn.

"What the hell do *you* want?" His breath smelled of the marijuana he'd smoked himself to sleep with.

"I'm a detective," I told him, making sure my jacket hung

open, showing my holstered gun. "There are a few questions for you to answer."

"Detective?" He lost some of his sleepiness. But he didn't look afraid, just interested. "Did I do something rash?"

"Somebody did," I said. "Mind if I come in?" I started in before he could answer, and he had to back up for me.

I closed the door behind me and looked around. The place was an enormous, cluttered room that served as artist's studio, bedroom and dining room. Most of the paintings that I could see were of faces, many of them children's faces. From what I could judge by the fitful fight of a single small lamp, the paintings were very good, each catching something unusual about the personality behind the face.

Arnie Sherwin watched me looking at his work. "Like?"

"Very much."

"You would," he said disgustedly. "A detective. You *know* anything about art?"

"Not much."

"That's how it is. Everybody that doesn't know likes what I do. And the lousy art critics and the pimps that run the galleries hate it. I do representational, and that's out of vogue. Nonobjective art is what they all go for now. Like a pack of lemmings. You're not supposed to know how to draw anymore. A guy throwing handfuls of paint at a canvas from twenty feet away—*that's* art these days. Nobody buys what I do. But I refuse to run with the pack."

"So you sketch caricatures at nightclubs and parties to earn your bread."

"Yes. That's what I do for a living." He said it as though admitting he had a social disease. "If I had the courage, I'd have stolen a sackful of money from the bank before I quit, like I wanted to."

"You were a banker?"

"Bank teller. Surprised? Hell, I was a solid citizen. In Denver. Job in a bank, wife, two lads, split-level outside the city—the whole suburban bit. Till two years ago. Then I just walked out on it all."

"The Gauguin bit," I said.

He laughed. Not happily. "You dig." He rubbed his murky eyes with his fingertips. "What'd you want to ask me, officer? I need sleep."

"You were at a party Gretchen Forrest threw at her house last Tuesday night."

He nodded. "So?"

"What time did you join the party?"

"I didn't join it. I never join. I go because I'm paid to be a source of amusement. And I don't remember what time I went. I was trying to earn a buck doing sketches in a club over on the Beach, the Padded Door. Danny Yale came in, drumming up people for this party at the Forrest place. He figured I'd be good for some laughs, so he slipped me a fifty to come along with the crowd."

If Arnie Sherwin knew about Yale being dead, it didn't interest him enough to mention it.

"Was Larry Score with Yale?" I asked him.

"No. Score was out finding other people for the blowout, like Yale was. But we ran into him, the last place Yale hit before heading for the Forrest place. We made quite a parade. Yale had more than a dozen cars packed with people trailing him. Score had almost as many. Gretchen Forrest was supposed to be waiting for us all with open arms. But by the time we got there, she'd gotten herself so drunk she couldn't have cared less if we were Martians. She cut out on the party right after we barged in on her. Went up to her room to sleep it off. The bash went on without her. And on and on. A real mess. Still going when I cut out. Around four in the morning, I guess."

"Do you know a woman named Sondra Lomax?" I asked him.

"I've seen her around. Works at Yale's club."

"Was she waiting with Gretchen Forrest when you got there?"

Arnie Sherwin shook his head. "She was supposed to be. Yale said he and Score left her there to wait with Gretchen Forrest. But by the time we all barged in, she'd cut out. There was just the Forrest dame and this gangster that pals around with her, Al Mungo. Mungo said Sondra got tired of waiting for us, and left. Yale kidded Larry Score about it. Said that'd teach Score to play one of his girlfriends against the other and get them fighting."

"Did Al Mungo stay at the party?" I asked.

"Not for too long," Arnie Sherwin said. "After Gretchen cut out, he said he had something to do. He had that big boat of his at the Forrest dock. He took Danny Yale and Score along with him and went off in it somewhere."

"Was Mungo's son at the party?"

"Didn't see him there."

"How about Mungo's mistress? Audrey."

"Not her, either."

"Could either of them have been there, and you just didn't notice?"

"I'd have noticed. I had to do sketches of just about every damn person at the party before they let me go."

"Was Kit Forrest there?"

"Gretchen's kid sister? She came in just before I escaped. But she didn't join. Not her kind of party."

I tried other questions on him, but they didn't add anything to the facts he'd given me.

As I turned to leave, Arnie Sherwin said, "I don't suppose you're going to tell me what this is all about. Are you?"

"No," I told him. "I'm not."

He shrugged, and I left.

I strode back to Kit's Jaguar. There were just a couple of more items I needed from the night, and my time was running out.

22.

THE LUCKY SEVEN WAS IN HIALEAH, near the track. Its neon sign had been shut off, but the entrance door wasn't locked. I went in cautiously. The interior was a long, wide room with a tiny stage at one end for the strippers. The walls were decorated with paintings of dice, cards, roulette wheels, horses and racing dogs. The Lucky Seven's trade was always liberally sprinkled with men who'd been winners at the track.

There was no trade in the Lucky Seven when I entered. Only a couple lightbulbs burned. It was closing time. By that time of morning, any loaded night owls that still hadn't had their fill had drifted over to Miami Beach. The janitor was mopping the floor and stacking chairs on the tables. Five B-girls were at the bar, looking limp and weary as they counted the swizzle sticks in their glasses. That was how the count was kept of their nightly earnings. Each B-girl got a percentage on each drink she managed to cadge from a customer. The bar cashier kept a separate glass for each girl under the bar, and dropped a swizzle stick into it to represent a cadged drink. In some joints, they kept track by using different-color swizzle sticks for each girl. A bottle of champagne earned a girl quite a lot of swizzle sticks, which was why they were always trying to wheedle, needle or trick the suckers into buying one.

The bar cashier was watching the swizzle-stick count with

suspicious eyes, while the bartender washed glasses in the sink. Several men lounged together at the end of the bar, but they weren't customers. They belonged to several of the B-girls. They watched the swizzle-stick count as closely as the cashier.

Two of the girls looked at me—weary-faced but prepared to earn themselves a few more swizzle sticks. I shook my head at them and they went back to counting. I asked the bartender, "Where's Morrie?"

"Upstairs. You want—"

"I know the way," I told him, and strode the length of the bar to a curtained doorway. It was more than a year since I'd been in the Lucky Seven. Long enough for none of the employees in the barroom to know me, not long enough for the setup of the place to have changed. I went through the doorway and up a short flight of stairs. Before I opened the door at the top, I took the gun from my belt holster. Morrie would know me.

I stepped inside quickly, shut the door behind me. Morrie was washing his face with cold water from the sink in one corner of his decrepit office. The door in the opposite wall was open, showing his disordered sleeping quarters. Morrie straightened with a towel in his hands, blinked his protruding eyes at me without recognition while his skinny, pinch-featured face dripped water.

"Get your glasses on, Morrie," I said.

He recognized my voice. Shock opened his mouth and deepened the wrinkles gouged in his cheeks. Dropping the towel, he fumbled for his glasses on the shelf over the sink, put them on his still-wet face. He blinked at me through their thick lenses, confirming what he'd heard.

"Rome! My God! What're you doing here? The cops're—"

"I know about the cops," I told him, cutting him short. "I need some help."

"From *me?* Don't expect it. I'm not sticking my—"

I raised the gun in my hand. He noticed it for the first time. He didn't say anything for a few seconds.

Then he said, in a pleading voice, "Don't be a hard guy, Rome.

You know I can't do anything to help you. I hide you out or something, and I'm in as much trouble as you. And believe me, you're in trouble. Killing a—"

"I don't need a hideout," I said. "You still steering dough-heavy customers to Mike Ryan's poker games?"

He answered "Uh huh" before he had time to think better of it.

"Where's Ryan got his game this morning?"

Morrie licked his lips, shook his head. "I dunno. Him and me had a fight. I don't steer for him anymore."

I moved in on him. "Morrie, I've already got a murder rap on me. They can't execute me twice."

He scrubbed trembling hands over the front of his shirt. "What do you want Ryan for?" he stalled.

I jammed the muzzle of the .38 into his gut. Not very hard. But he bent over, moaning and clutching where I'd jabbed him, leaning a hip against the sink for support.

"Jesus!" he gasped when he was able. "You hadn't ought to've done that! I got an ulcer inside here!"

"You've got mush in there," I told him softly. "You know you're going to have to do what I want. If you don't, I'll start by making mincemeat of your face with this gun."

He straightened, forgetting his pretense of great agony. He put a shaky hand on the sink and said, low, "Mike Ryan ain't got a game this morning. He took a day off. Got a new girlfriend."

"Then you know where he's staying with her."

An attempt at cunning showed in his slitted eyes. "I—ain't sure."

"Get sure. Or get hurt."

He sighed. "They're shacked up in a hotel over on Biscayne Boulevard."

"Phone him," I ordered Morrie. "Tell him to come over here."

"Here? Now?"

"Right now."

"But he's with a *girl*. How'll I get him—"

"You'll figure out something," I told him. "Because if you

can't, you're no help to me. And I might as well kill you."

"Don't talk like that. Even for a joke."

I looked at him. His eyes slid away from mine, toward the wall. But there was a mirror there, over the sink, and he could see me looking at him in it.

He took his hand from the sink. "Okay," he said weakly. "I'll try. Maybe he'll understand I had to. Maybe." He walked to his desk, a skinny and mournful man carrying a fate too heavy for him on his narrow shoulders.

As he picked up his phone with his right hand, his other hand drifted as though by accident toward the middle drawer of his desk.

"Do you really want to try it?" I said softly.

His left hand jumped away from the drawer. He took a deep breath and stuck out a finger to dial the phone.

"Where are you calling?" I asked him pointedly.

"The hotel," Morrie said innocently. "Where—"

"The hotel has a name."

He told it to me. I got the phone book from under his desk, looked up the hotel.

"Now dial," I told him.

If he'd had it in mind to dial the cops, or anyone else, he resigned himself to the fact that it wasn't going to work. I watched him dial the hotel's number. He asked for Michael Ryan, had his story ready when Ryan answered his room phone.

"This is Morrie," he told Ryan through the phone. He didn't have to fake the urgency in his voice. The gun pointing at him gave his voice everything it needed to be convincing. "That cop's back again. The one who . . . . Sure he got the dough. But he says he needs more all've a sudden. Emergency . . . He won't tell me. . . . Sure I told him it wasn't right. But he won't listen to me. He says he wants more dough or he breaks into your next game. And he wants to see you. Here. Right away—"

Morrie put down the phone, wiped his perspiring face. "He hung up on me!"

"Is he coming?" I demanded tightly.

Morrie nodded. "But he's sore. He's gonna be sorer when he finds out." Morrie dropped into the chair behind his desk.

I sat in another chair beside his desk, turned it so I could look at him and the door. "Don't worry about Ryan," I told him. "He'll be relieved that I'm not a cop after a graft raise. Just worry about *me,* and behave yourself."

He behaved himself. When the cashier came up with the night's take, Morrie played it straight—while I sat there holding the gun in my pocket and the smile on my face. Morrie took the cash box and ledger, told the cashier to leave the back door open because he was expecting more company.

After the cashier left, I took the gun out of my pocket and stripped off the eye patch. With a man like Mike Ryan, it was best to use both eyes.

Ryan arrived fifteen minutes after the cashier left. He opened the door without knocking. I stood up fast, backing up so I could keep the gun on him and Morrie. Ryan was calmer than I was. His poker face didn't alter a hair when he saw me and the gun. He closed the door quietly behind him, let both arms dangle full length at his sides so I wouldn't get nervous. He was a trim, beautifully tailored man with silver hair and silvery-gray eyes that looked like they spent most of their time in a deep-freeze unit.

He turned those eyes briefly on Morrie. The man at the desk put his hands together and pointed them at Ryan as though he were praying to him. "I couldn't help it, Ryan! You see how it is. He's got a gun."

Ryan looked at me and nodded. "I see it. What do you want, Rome? If it's money to get away—"

"No. Information is all I need from you."

He raised and lowered his padded shoulders. "If I can give it, without endangering myself."

There was no need for threats with Mike Ryan. He was bright enough to know the danger of a desperate man with a gun.

"Earl Gronsky held up a game you were running a couple years back," I said. "Just before he was caught and sent up. Who was in that game?"

"The game was over when Gronsky walked in on us," Ryan told me. "Everyone had gone-except myself and the big winner."

"Al Mungo," I said.

Ryan nodded. "We were having a last drink together. Mungo was in a high mood. Then Gronsky kicked in the door and walked in with a gun in his hand. Mungo told him who he was. It didn't impress Gronsky. He even thought it was funny, taking money from a man like Mungo."

"How much did he take?"

"Everything we had with us. Almost nine thousand dollars from me. Everything Mungo had started the game with, plus all he'd won. Which came to a hundred and sixty-seven thousand dollars."

I whistled softly. All that money, and I was the only one who knew where it was. The only catch being that I was in no position to go get it.

"What did Mungo do about it?" I asked Ryan. Ryan thought about answering, apparently could find no harm in telling me. "Mungo set out to get Gronsky and the money, of course. The difficulty was that Gronsky was in hiding, had been for quite some time. The cops were after him for a number of big jobs he'd pulled. But Mungo had an ace in the hole. Gronsky was crazy about some girl. And the girl was crazy about one of Mungo's boys."

"Larry Score," I said.

"Yes," Ryan said. "Score. Mungo gave Score the job of finding out if the girl knew where Gronsky was holed up. In case she did, he sent a hood named Kay along with Score. The two of them were to get Gronsky, get the money back from him."

"And kill Gronsky," I added.

Ryan nodded.

"Why didn't Mungo send Frenchy and Shev along, too?"

"He didn't have them working for him two years ago. Just Larry Score. And Kay sometimes did jobs for him. Mungo was playing at being retired a bit harder in those days."

"Score and Kay have any luck?"

Ryan shrugged a shoulder. "The cops got Gronsky before Score could worm out of the girl whether she knew where Gronsky was."

"Mungo tried to get Gronsky again when he got out of prison earlier this week," I said.

"So I heard. He's bound to get Gronsky eventually. Gronsky is crazy, or he'd have realized that."

"I guess you're pretty anxious to get even with Gronsky, too," I suggested.

"I've been heisted before," Ryan said calmly. "I will be again. It's a hazard of my profession. A gambler is a natural for that sort of thing. He can't holler for the cops. The nine thousand didn't break me. I could take it more philosophically than Mungo."

"Who killed Danny Yale?" I asked, trying a sudden switch.

It didn't bother him. "I heard you did."

"You always believe what you hear?"

"Unless I hear something different. Didn't you kill him?" Ryan's usefulness was ended. I had what I'd wanted from him. I motioned with the .38. "Over against that wall."

Ryan moved away from the door.

"You, too, Morrie."

Morrie joined Ryan against the wall. "I know you won't do anything to stop me," I said to Ryan. "Make sure Morrie doesn't, either." I went to the door, took the key out of the lock. Going out of the office, I locked the door from the outside. They'd give me a little time before making the noise required to break the door open. I hurried down the steps. The club was empty, lit only by a single bulb behind the bar. I used the back door.

I put the eye patch back on before driving the white Jaguar back to the island containing the Forrest villa. I had to use the causeway, and there were cops guarding the Miami end of it. But they were watching for anyone coming *from* Miami Beach, not going toward it. They looked at me as I drove onto the causeway. But the combination of the black eye patch and the white sports car prevented them from giving me serious thought.

I stopped the Jaguar as soon as I got off the causeway onto the little residential island. I walked the rest of the way along the edge of the inner driveway, following it to my left to avoid passing Mungo's place.

The first graying of the predawn was in the sky. Kit Forrest would be asleep by now. I was glad that her sleeping quarters were soundproofed. I was going to waken Gretchen and have a talk with her. It was likely to get noisy. I didn't want Kit to witness what her helping me was going to do to her sister.

23

I DIDN'T HAVE TO WAKE GRETCHEN FORREST. She hadn't gone to sleep yet. I found her slumped on the couch in her vast living room, trying to drink herself into oblivion with a tumblerful of whisky. The room was in shadow except for a small area lighted by the lamp beside the couch. I stood there observing her without her seeing me—long enough to see that she'd been at the drinking for quite a while.

"It won't help," I said quietly.

She raised her head and looked at me. My presence didn't startle her. I was just another in a procession of nightmarish visions she'd been contemplating.

"I took some pills, too," she said, forcing out each word separately. "They'll work. Eventually."

"They'll wear off. Eventually. Then it will be back with you."

A shred of cunning struggled to the surface in her. "*What* will be back with me?"

I lowered my hip to the wide arm of a wing chair, not fully entering the light from the lamp. The shadows masked my face from her. "Other people have it easier than you," I said carefully. "When they sin, they have to take their punishment. And it cleanses them. But your money's always bought you out of trouble. And that way you can never really get the trouble out of you. It stays with you. You have to live with it the rest of your life, suffering while it tears your insides."

She raised her glass to her slack mouth. But she couldn't drink from it. With a moan of despair, she threw the glass. It smashed to splinters on the marble floor. Her head lolled back on top of the couch and she stared up at the shadowed ceiling.

"Tell me," I urged softly. "It's the only way to get it out of you. Hold this one in and it'll tear you apart."

A sound came out of her—a long sigh punctuated by a descending succession of dry sobs.

"I already know most of it," I told her. "So you can't do yourself any further damage by telling me all of it. Holding it in will do you more harm."

Her head rolled on the top of the couch till she was looking at me through the shadows. Her lips moved, but no words came out.

I had to start it for her. "You fought with Sondra Lomax, over Larry Score. You thought he was yours. But when you all came here Tuesday night, Sondra acted possessive about him. And Larry Score acted as though he couldn't make up his mind between you. You were all drinking. The four of you, including Danny Yale. Then Score and Yale went out to find people for a big shindig. After they'd gone, you and Sondra fought over Score. And you stabbed her to death."

I waited, watching Gretchen Forrest. She didn't say anything. She acted as though she were too far gone to hear me. But she heard me.

"When you realized what you'd done," I went on slowly, "you panicked. You did what's become second nature for you. You're used to having others pull you out of the holes you fall into. You called Al Mungo. He thought you had a magic key that would let him enter the world of monied respectability. You knew you could count on him. He came over here, hid Sondra's body before Score and Yale showed up with the crowd for your party. Then he told them what had happened. The three of them gave the party the slip, took Sondra Lomax out on Mungo's boat. Dropped her in the ocean after hardening a box of cement around her feet."

Gretchen struggled to get up, changed her mind and leaned forward, hunching down with her elbows on her knees and her face buried in the palms of her hands.

"Tell me," I said insistently. "It's the only way to stop the consequences. There's already been too many of those. And there'll be more, unless you stop it. I imagine you think the killing of Sondra Lomax was an accident. But the killing of Maria Barreto wasn't. It was deliberate, premeditated murder."

Gretchen raised her distorted face from her hands and stared at me blankly. "Who is Maria Barreto?"

"So Mungo didn't tell you about her," I mused aloud. "You're responsible for her death nevertheless. She was Sondra's roommate. Mungo had her strangled to death to stop her from saying anything that might put me and the cops on your trail for the killing of Sondra. He had Danny Yale murdered for the same reason."

Sharp, deep lines appeared between Gretchen's eyebrows. "Al Mungo killed Danny?"

"Had him killed. I was pressuring Yale. Maybe it was making Yale too nervous to be trusted. By framing the murder on me, Mungo could get me out of his hair without actually killing me— the way I'd told the police he was trying to. So there's three people so far paying the consequences for you—Maria Barreto, Danny Yale and me. And it won't end with us. Unless *you* end it. Mungo's gotten himself in too deep, trying to help you out. He can't afford to let anyone potentially dangerous to him live. The next one who'll be dangerous to him is—your sister."

"Kit?"

"She knows I didn't kill Yale. She won't stand still for my taking the rap for it."

"Why should Kit—"

"Because we're in love with each other," I lied flatly. Love for the wrong man was something she could understand, something calculated to touch her most deeply.

176

"You're lying!" Gretchen spat. But there was no conviction behind the words.

I shook my head. "How do you think I've evaded the police this long? I've been in Kit's bedroom almost the whole time." I described Kit's quarters in detail for her.

Gretchen groaned thinly.

"Tell me," I said again softly. "Or would you rather let your own sister take the consequences for you?"

She swayed to her feet and pressed the tips of her fingers against her temples. "All right!" she moaned. "I killed Sondra!"

I let my breath out slowly. "Tell me," I repeated.

"We were quarreling over Larry. I—I got quite violent about it. And Larry acted as though it were all a big joke. I drank too much, too fast. I got drunk."

She swayed again. I stood up quickly, ready to catch her.

But she didn't fall. "I—don't remember it all very well. Too much to drink. After Larry and Danny left I—" She shook her head as though to clear it of fog. "I'm not sure exactly how it happened. I guess Sondra and I got more violent when we were left together. The next thing I knew—she was lying there." Gretchen pointed at the floor in front of the couch. "She was dead. I was slumped on the couch."

Gretchen moved with slow, uncertain steps to a leather-covered little desk, picked up a sharp, long-bladed letter opener from it. "I had this in my hand—with her blood all over it. I'd stabbed her with it."

She raised the letter opener. The long, thin blade projecting downward from her fist caught the lamplight and seemed to glisten with an evil life of its own. Gretchen raised her fist and slashed the blade downward slowly, staring at it. "I stabbed her," she repeated in a whisper. "But I didn't mean to—I didn't want to."

She opened her fingers. The deadly letter opener rang on the marble floor by her feet.

"You claim you don't remember doing it," I said.

"I *don't*. I was so drunk—I must have blacked out, not realized what I was doing. That *happens,* doesn't it?"

"Yes," I said. "It happens that way. Sometimes."

There was only one more piece left to be fitted into place. I strode to the phone on a little table beside a curtained archway. Picked it up and dialed the home number of Hal Rubin, my friend in the sheriff's office.

Rubin picked up his phone on the third ring. "Wha'?" he mumbled into the phone, fighting his way up out of sleep.

"This is Rome," I told him.

"Tony?" The sleep fled from his voice. "Where are you?"

"I'll tell you in a moment," I said. "First I need—"

"You listen to me, Tony," he cut in, talking fast. "You know I'm your friend. I wouldn't give you a wrong steer. For your own good, give yourself up. If you killed—"

"I didn't. You know damn well I didn't."

"Whether you did or didn't," Rubin snapped, "you've got to give yourself up. Running away only makes you look guiltier. There's only one way to clear yourself. Come in and tell us the facts. Please, Tony. As your friend, I beg you. Wherever you are, let me come and get you. I swear—"

"I'm going to do just that," I told him through the phone. "But first you have to tell me one thing. That anonymous phone tip your office got two years ago—the one telling you where to find Earl Gronsky. Was it a man or a woman that called in the tip?"

"A man. Where are you, Tony?"

"I'll call you back," I said, and hung up the phone.

I turned back to Gretchen Forrest.

She was no longer looking at me.

She was looking at Al Mungo.

24.

MUNGO STOOD BESIDE THE COUCH. The .38 revolver in his fist had a silencer attachment. It was pointed at me. His ears had never seemed so long and pointed. His gash of a mouth had never been so frightening.

"I been worried about you, Gretchen," Mungo said through his teeth, not taking his eyes off me. "You been acting like you're losing your grip. So I hid a microphone behind those curtains there. Had it hooked to a speaker in my study so I could hear if you went off your rocker all the way. Lucky I did it. Lucky I was up to hear you spilling your lousy guts."

"Come to do your dirty work yourself?" I asked him tightly. "What happened to all your hired help?"

"They're out doing a job for me. They'll be back. You think I can't take care've you myself? How do you think I got where I am?"

"Stealing pennies from babies."

The gash of a mouth became thinner, longer. "Crack wise, Rome. Go ahead. I grew up with a gun in my fist. Next wrong word or move outa you, I put a slug through your left eye. It won't touch bone till it hits the back've your skull."

I held myself very still.

Mungo said, "Take out your gun. Use two fingers of your left hand. Not the thumb. Toss it away behind you."

Nerves along the lengths of my fingers were jumping as I

unbuttoned my jacket, pulled it away from the belt holster.

"I'm gonna kill you anyhow," Mungo informed me quietly. "Try something and we'll do it here and now. It wouldn't be any problem for me any more. Not with the cops after you for murder. I just have you dumped in the ocean, after. And the cops figure you ran outa the state."

His eyes and gun watched me get two fingers of my left hand around the butt of my gun, tug it out of the holster. There was a split second in which I considered throwing my life away on the thin chance of taking him with me. But I threw the gun away; instead.

"Nice," Mungo whispered. And then his free hand lashed out and slammed across Gretchen Forrest's face.

She fell over the arm of the couch, her face flaming from the blow. Considering the obvious pain, it brought a very small cry from her.

"You deserved that," Mungo rasped. He no longer looked calm. His face was twisted with rage.

Gretchen sat up on the couch, pressing a hand against her hurt cheek. 'I don't deserve *anything,*" she whispered raggedly.

"I got into this mess on account of *you,*" Mungo snarled at Gretchen. "You kill a girl and come begging me for help. Didn't I help when you needed it? I went in deep for your sake, damn you! Not just dumping Sondra in the water for you. Next I had to have that Barreto girl killed. For you. And then Danny. Yale's no loss. He was holding out dough from the club on me. He was due to get it anyway. But the rest've it ... *all for you. I* risk everything I got for you. And now you turn on me."

His face was the face of a lover betrayed. I'd once seen that kind of rage in another man. A man who'd given up wife, children, home and a fortune in alimony for a woman—only to have that woman decide she didn't really want him after all.

"What am I supposed to do with you now?" Mungo whispered.

He was still watching me, but the question was for Gretchen Forrest. She didn't answer.

"I can't trust you any more," Mungo whispered. "And now it's *my* neck I got to look out for. All on account of I tried to save yours."

He slipped his left hand in his jacket pocket, motioned to me with the gun. "We take a walk down to the water."

Gretchen took her hand away from her face. "What are you going to do to him?" she demanded.

"Shut up," he warned her. "All you do now is wait till I get back."

"I don't want anybody else killed because of me!" she pleaded. "I didn't ask you to kill *anybody.*"

"No," Mungo snarled. "All you wanted was for me to cover up a murder for you. How'd you think it was done—with mirrors?" He motioned at me again, sharply. "I said *walk.*"

I walked. Slowly. I went past them, toward the pool area behind the villa. There was a sharp sound of something hard striking flesh-covered bone behind me. I whirled.

Gretchen sprawled unconscious on the floor in front of the couch. Mungo stood over her, brass knuckles jutting from his clenched left fist. His eyes and gun jumped back to me.

"Now," he said, "she'll wait. Till I take care of you." He came around the couch toward me. "Move."

Slowly, I turned my back to him. He followed me out to the rear terrace. I began to get my hopes up as I saw how dark it was beyond the other end of the swimming pool.

But Mungo saw it, too. "Stop right there," he hissed.

I stopped. My spine cringed in expectation of a bullet.

"This'll do," Mungo said behind me. "I can drag you the rest've the way."

"Wait," I said quickly. "I'm the only one knows where the money is."

"Money?"

"The hundred and sixty-seven thousand dollars Gronsky took off you. Kill me and you'll never find it."

"I'll still have Gronsky," Mungo said behind me. "That's

where my boys are. Getting him outa that hospital."

"They'll play hell trying to take Gronsky."

"With a broken leg? And no gun on him? The three've 'em can take him like that."

"He's got a police guard on him."

"One cop. The cop'll take a walk to the bathroom. He'll take his time there. By the time he gets back, Gronsky's gone."

"Enough money will buy you anything," I acknowledged. "The only problem is Gronsky won't tell you where your hundred and sixty-seven thousand is. He wouldn't if he could. And he can't. He doesn't know. I'm the only one who does."

"Keep talking," Mungo said. There was a little hesitation in his voice now.

"Gronsky hid the dough in a boat he gave to Sondra Lomax. She didn't know about it. And she sank the boat in an accident, while he was in prison. I know exactly where the boat was sunk."

"If the dough's been in the water long," Mungo growled, "then it's all ruined."

"Gronsky would have wrapped the money in something waterproof," I said. "Everything on a boat gets wet, sooner or later. If—"

The rest of what I had to say was cut short by a burst of agony behind my ear as Mungo's brass knuckles struck.

I tried to turn, but my legs weren't there. I fell through darkness. By the time I landed, none of me was there.

I didn't want to open my eyes. My head ached horribly, and I knew it would feel worse when I was fully awake. But some small, dim part of my fragmented brain kept telling me there was a reason to open my eyes. A reason like the difference between living and dying. I opened my eyes.

I looked up at Audrey. The only light out there on the patio behind Mungo's house came from inside the house. But even in that shadowy light, there was no mistaking the figure of Mungo's mistress. Even in a billowy nightgown.

She stood over me, staring down at me, puzzled. I lay on my side on the hard patio. My wrists were handcuffed behind me. My ankles were bound tightly together with rope. Adhesive tape was plastered over my mouth.

"What are you doing here?" Audrey demanded softly.

I made as much sound as I could through the gag.

She squatted beside me, ripped the tape off my face.

"Where's Mungo?" I asked, fast and soft.

"I don't know. I was looking for him when—Who *are* you?"

"Get something to cut these ropes," I said quickly. "And a key for these cuffs."

She shook her head. "I couldn't do that. Al might—"

"You'd *better,*" I told her tensely. "Or I'll tell Mungo how you've been playing around behind his back—with his own son."

Even in that dim light I had no trouble seeing the terror that twisted in her like a knife.

"By the way," I said, "where *is* Paul?"

"Visiting a friend for a couple . . . . It's not true! What you say about me and—"

"Sure it is. And I wouldn't have much trouble making Mungo know it. You and his son. Paul got Kit Forrest to cover up for him each time the two of you snuck out to meet somewhere. But she won't cover up for him any more. Mungo won't do much to his own son. Even for something like that. But you—he'll cut pieces out of your face with a red-hot butcher knife."

She shot to her feet, fists pressed against her mouth. "No," she whispered. "Please don't—"

"On the other hand," I said, talking fast and praying Mungo would take his time, wherever he'd gone, "if you get me loose, I'll most likely have to kill Mungo. Then you won't have anything to worry about. You'll have Paul—and Paul will have all his father's dough."

She frowned, hesitating, chewing her ripe lower lip.

I didn't have the time. "Better make up your mind fast," I prodded her. "Before Mungo gets back. It'll be too late then—for both of us."

She turned suddenly, hurried off into the house. I lay on the hard patio waiting, trying to judge the passage of time by the pulse of my heart. But the beat was too abnormal to judge by.

Her slippers whispered over the patio as she hurried back out of the house.

"I don't know where the key is," she whispered. "But I got a razor blade."

"Get my legs loose. Hurry." At least I'd be able to run for it. She started to bend to me, froze at the sound of footsteps hurrying toward the patio from the bay shore. She straightened quickly as Al Mungo came up onto the patio. She dropped the razor blade. It made a tiny clinking sound on the patio beside me. I wriggled over on my elbows and closed my right hand around the little blade, praying he hadn't heard it fall.

He hadn't. "What're *you* doing out here?" he growled at his platinum-haired mistress.

"I woke up and wondered where you were," she said shakily. "I came out looking for you."

Then Mungo saw that my gag was off. He took another step toward Audrey. "What the hell were you doing with *him*?"

"I—I found him here. I didn't know who he was or—What's going on?"

Mungo studied her intently. Finally he snapped, "Get back inside. Forget about it. And I do mean *forget*. Go to bed and stay there."

She muttered, "Sure, Al. Sure." She gave me a last, pleading glance and ran into the house, the sheer nightgown billowing out behind her.

Al Mungo stared after her meditatively. Then he looked down at me, knelt on one knee and tested the ropes binding my ankles together. Satisfied that they hadn't been tampered with, he rolled me over on my face. I clenched both hands into fists behind my back. The razor blade sliced into my palm, but it was better than his seeing it and taking it away from me.

He made sure the handcuffs were still locked, stood up.

"You got a hard skull, Rome. I didn't figure on you coming to so quick."

"What'd you do to Gretchen Forrest?"

"Nothing. Yet. Just carried her to my boat. She's still out. I'll wait for Larry and the boys to get here with Gronsky and let them carry you aboard. It was hard enough lugging you this far."

"And when we're all on your boat?"

"We all go for a ride. We go out and get my dough. Maybe you think you won't help me find it. But you will. Sooner or later."

"I guess I will," I admitted. "And then?"

"Don't be in such a rush," Al Mungo told me softly. "The little time you got left to you, you want to just live each minute as it comes along."

25.

LATE-MORNING SUN SCORCHED DOWN on the empty sea all around us as Mungo's long, sleek cabin cruiser rolled on the swells half a mile off Elliot Key. There were seven of us in the open cockpit, but we didn't crowd it.

Gretchen Forrest sat in one of the swivel fishing chairs, her wrists tied to its arms. She gazed off at the distant horizon, lost in her own miserable thoughts, seeming to have lost all interest in what was happening and what was likely to happen—to her or anybody else.

I sat on the deck, leaning against the bulwark with my legs bent back under me, my wrists still cuffed together and my ankles still bound by the ropes. Gronsky sat beside me, his wrists tied behind him with rope, his good leg and the one in the cast sticking straight out on the deck. They'd knocked him out with a lead pipe before taking him from the hospital. He'd been conscious for over an hour, stoically bearing the agony in his smashed leg. They'd handled him roughly, carrying him—and then had beaten on his cast with the lead pipe in an effort to make him tell exactly where on the boat he'd hidden the money. He hadn't told them.

Larry Score leaned against the opposite gunwale, across the cockpit, guarding us with a .44 Magnum in his hand. Al Mungo sat in the twin of Gretchen's chair, impatiently watching Frenchy strap a fresh tank of air on Shev's back. Shev had been under a long time, looking for the sunken boat. By the time he'd located it, he had too little air left to search the wreck for the money.

Frenchy finished the job, and Shev pulled his face mask back on, took the mouthpiece between his teeth. Frenchy made sure the rubber bag that was to carry the money was securely attached to Shev's weight belt. Then Shev, walking awkwardly in his rubber fins, went to the ladder that hung over the port side into the water. He carried a powerful speargun, in case he ran into a shark or barracuda below.

As he climbed down the ladder, everyone watched him. Behind my back, I hacked away with the razor blade at the ropes binding my ankles. There'd been three of them, each separately knotted. It had been slow, difficult work, trying to cut through while being watched every second. I'd only managed to cut one of the ropes till then.

But by the time Shev vanished into the water and everybody stopped looking at him, I'd slashed through the second rope. That left one to go.

Mungo looked at me. "The dough better be in that boat like you said, Rome. If it ain't, I'll tear your tongue out with a pair of pliers."

"It's there," I assured him. "Shev's bound to find it, in a boat that small."

I was working on the last rope tying my ankles. It was desperately slow work, with them watching me again. I had to cut it a thin fiber at a time, sawing the blade back and forth just a fraction of an inch each time.

Gronsky turned his head and looked at me. "You yellow fink," he said, for maybe the third time since he'd come to. "Why'd you have to tell 'em where the boat was?"

I shrugged. "Why not? The dough won't do either of *us* any good, where we're going."

"So'd you have to let *them* have it?"

"They'd have gotten the truth out of us eventually, anyway."

"Out've *you,* you mean," Gronsky stated disgustedly. "You crack like an eggshell soon's they squeeze you a little."

Larry Score laughed. "You sound like you enjoyed being squeezed, Gronsky. Want me to beat on that cast of yours some more with the lead pipe?"

"Sure," Gronsky growled. "Only this time try it without three other guys holding me down. Just you."

Score's lips thinned back from his teeth, and suddenly he didn't look handsome at all. He took a step toward Gronsky, raising the gun in his hand threateningly.

"Stop it!" Mungo barked at him. "Leave 'em alone till we know if the dough's there."

Larry Score leaned back against the gunwale, staring at Gronsky and me. "It'll be a pleasure taking care of you two. I'll do it with a knife."

"Sure you will," I said. "That's your style." I was halfway through the last rope. My fingers were sweating with the need to hurry and not being able to hurry. Whenever Shev surfaced with that money, I'd be all out of time. I had to be ready. I had to get their eyes off me, for a short time at least.

I looked at Al Mungo. "How's it feel," I asked him, "to be played for a sucker? A big man like you?"

Mungo's eyes narrowed. After a moment he looked away from me, at Gretchen Forrest. "She'll pay for it," he said tonelessly.

Frenchy and Score looked at Gretchen, too. I dug the razor blade deeper into the rope.

"Why should *she* pay?" I said. "She's in the same boat you are, Mungo. You were both suckered. By the one who murdered Sondra Lomax."

Gretchen removed her eyes from the horizon and stared at me blankly.

"No," I told her quietly, "*you* didn't kill Sondra. That's why you can't remember doing it."

"But—I—" It took her an effort to get her voice under control. "I—stabbed her. With the letter opener. She was dead at my feet, and I—"

"All you can remember was arguing with her, and being very drunk. The next thing you can remember, Sondra was dead and you had the weapon that had killed her in your hand. Between those two memories, you've got a blackout. Not a psychological blackout, as you assumed. You *passed* out."

"Passed out?"

"Uh huh. From the dope Larry Score put in your drink to give him time to kill Sondra Lomax and stick the murder weapon in your hand."

I looked back at Mungo. "*That's* who's played you for a sucker, from start to finish. Your *boy*. Larry Score."

I looked at Score and saw I was about to die. His handsome face looked sick and he was turning his Magnum on me and there was no doubt about what he intended doing with it.

"Larry!" Al Mungo's voice slashed Score like a whip.

Score turned his head stiffly, slowly. He saw the .38 that had appeared in Mungo's hand, aimed at him.

"Drop it, Larry. Or I'll put a slug in your shoulder."

Mungo said it without moving his lips. He might have been a ventriloquist's dummy for all he seemed to have to do with the peculiar voice that came out of him. I'd never seen this Mungo before. I didn't believe Score had, either. This was a Mungo from long before, back in the days when he'd been killing his way up the Capone ladder of success during the Prohibition wars.

"He's lying!" Score blurted. "You know he is!"

"I know," Mungo said in that same strange, blood-chilling voice. "But I'm listening to what he's got to say. I want to hear it all. And I told you to drop it, Larry."

Score's gun sagged. But didn't drop.

Behind him, Frenchy took his gun from his belt. He touched the muzzle to Score's back. "You heard the boss, Larry," Frenchy said placatingly. "Be a good joe."

Score forced his fingers open. The .44 Magnum thudded to the deck. "Al—why listen to *him*? All he's trying to do is—"

"Be quiet awhile, Larry," Mungo told him, almost gently.

He glanced at me. "You got more to say, say it. If it ain't good, Larry can have you."

I had the last rope cut almost all the way through by then. But I had to stop sawing with the razor blade when Mungo and Frenchy and Score looked at me. The ways in which they looked at me differed. Mungo's look was coldly appraising. Frenchy was suspicious and curious. Larry Score was looking sicker by the second. And I knew I'd been right.

"My story's good," I assured Mungo. "Gretchen showed me how she thought she'd killed Sondra Lomax. She held the letter opener the way anybody except a knife expert would—with the blade stabbing downward. But that's not the way Sondra was killed. The blade went into Sondra just under the breastbone and was driven upward into her heart. That's not easy to do. It took an expert. Larry's the expert."

"Why would Larry kill Sondra?" Mungo asked quietly.

"The reason goes back over two years—to the time Gronsky here heisted all that money from you. You gave Score the job of finding out where Gronsky was holed up, and taking him. You figured Sondra was crazy enough about Score to tell him where Gronsky was. She did know. And she *did* tell Score. But there was one thing you didn't know, Mungo. Your boy Larry Score has a little yellow spot in him. And where Gronsky's concerned, he's all yellow."

"It's not true!" Score yelled. "He's just—"

"It's true all right," I said. "I'll get around to proving it by and by."

"You lying bastard, I'll—"

Mungo said, "I told you to be quiet awhile, Larry." He said it in a way that closed Score's mouth as though he'd been slapped.

"You see," I went on, "Score had tangled with Gronsky before. He had a gun and a knife, but Gronsky took them from him, barehanded. Then he put Score over his knee and cut his initials in Score's hide. That busted Score's confidence down so low it's never quite recovered. And when he thought about tackling Gronsky again—even with the help of Kay, the hood you sent with him—Score got the shakes. Because you wanted them to take Gronsky alive, long enough to make him tell where he had your money hidden. And Score knew he wouldn't live to get it done.

"So he figured out a way to put Gronsky where he couldn't be expected to get at him. He phoned the cops and told them where to find Gronsky. That way, *they* got him first. Score didn't have to tackle him, and he stayed aces with you."

Beside me, Gronsky made a growling sound, deep in his throat. I looked at him. "Yes, I know. You thought it was Sondra who tipped the cops where to find you. Because she was the only one who knew where you were holed up. But it wasn't a woman who phoned the tip to the cops. It was a man. And if Sondra was the only one who knew where you were, Score was the only man who could have learned it from her."

Gronsky looked at Score with a crazy kind of grin on his face.

I turned back to Mungo. "Score's idea went wrong in one way, though. With all the things the cops were waiting to pin on Gronsky, Score figured he'd be put away for at least twenty years. But the way it turned out, all they could make stick against Gronsky was a little gas-station job, and Gronsky got off with just three years in prison.

"And when Gronsky surprised him by getting paroled after only *two* years, Score knew he had to do something fast. Gronsky was bound to come after Sondra, ready to kill her for squealing on him. She'd have to tell him the truth to save her neck. And when Gronsky knew it was Score who tipped the cops about him, he'd come after Score.

"So Score figured out a way to murder Sondra before Gronsky got to her. A way that would leave him in the clear. Gretchen was gone on him, just like Sondra—and that made Gretchen the perfect one to take the fall for him. He planned it in detail, and he was in control every step of the way, last Tuesday night.

"He maneuvered it so that he and Yale wound up with

Gretchen and Sondra at Gretchen's house. They did a lot of drinking. With both girls getting loaded, it was no trick at all for Score to set the two of them to fighting over him. When it had gone far enough for his purpose, he suggested that he and Yale go out and pick up a crowd for a big party. And he doped Gretchen's drink before leaving.

"Outside Gretchen's house, Score and Yale split up to search for people for the party. With Yale gone, it was a simple matter for Score to slip back, watch through the window till he saw Gretchen pass out. Then he went inside, took up the letter opener and killed Sondra with it. She was probably dead before she realized what he was up to. And then all Score had to do was stick the murder weapon in Gretchen's hand and leave to go about the job of rounding up people for the party.

"It worked out with Gretchen the way Score had figured. She'd been very far gone on liquor before she took the doped drink. So when she came to and found Sondra dead at her feet, and the bloodstained murder weapon in her own hand, she assumed her quarrel with Sondra had become more violent—and ended with her killing Sondra.

"Score picked well in Gretchen. He knew she wouldn't take the fall. She had too much money and influence. And she had you, Mungo, to help her cover up the murder for her—for Score, really. She phoned you. You came over, got Sondra's body out to your boat and when Yale and Score arrived with the crowd, it was no problem for the three of you to leave the party, go out on your boat and get rid of Sondra Lomax. With a block of cement around her feet.

"But then I came along, and you had some problems, after all. By the way, who did the jobs on Maria Barreto and Yale for you?"

"Larry."

"Good old Larry. And all the time you thought he was working for you. When actually it was you who were working for him. He was using you. Like he used Gretchen. You both played his game like puppets on strings. And didn't even guess it. Till now."

Mungo watched me with absolutely no change of expression. "That all of it?" he asked tonelessly.

I nodded, waiting for them to stop looking at me so I could finish getting my ankles loose.

Mungo turned his eyes on Larry Score. "All right, Larry," he told him softly. "Now you can talk."

But the words didn't come right away. Score had to work at it to get them out. "What's there to say? He's lying, that's all. Just lies, start to finish. You know I—"

I interrupted him sharply. "It all hangs on one thing, really. Whether I'm lying about your being scared silly of Gronsky. It's easy to prove. Either way." I looked at Mungo. "Your boy's got a knife on him. Tell him to use it to cut Gronsky's wrists loose. Shouldn't worry a tough boy like Larry Score. He'll have the knife. Gronsky's got a useless leg and no weapon."

Mungo considered it, nodded slowly. "Go ahead, Larry. Cut Gronsky loose."

"That's crazy," Score blurted. "What—"

"Cut him loose."

Score didn't move. It was as though his joints had frozen and his feet were nailed to the deck. The flesh of his face seemed to have shrunk against the bones. He stared at Gronsky's crazy grin, and couldn't move.

"There's another way," I said. "Have Score let down his pants so we can see if Gronsky really did cut his initials in him."

"Larry . . . ?" Mungo whispered.

Score broke then. He dropped to one knee and grabbed at his fallen Magnum.

Mungo's .38 coughed. He hadn't been kidding about his ability with a gun. The .38 slug smashed into Score's right shoulder, driving through and shattering bones. Score fell over on his left side and curled up in a tight, sobbing ball, clutching at his terrible wound.

"I warned you, Larry," Mungo said softly.

But Larry Score didn't hear him. He was isolated from the rest of us in an ocean of sick pain. And as they all watched him, I cut through the last of the rope around my ankles.

"Look!" Frenchy yelled suddenly, and pointed over the starboard side. Shev had bobbed up to the surface. Mungo got off his chair, fast.

I slipped the razor blade behind Gronsky's back, touched his hand with it. He frowned, not registering what it was. I dug the sharp edge into his skin. He knew then. His fingers snatched the blade from mine.

In the water to starboard, Shev had raised an arm, was waving it back and forth.

"He's got the dough!" Frenchy shouted, grinning.

Shev dove back down under the surface to swim below the keel to the portside where the ladder was.

I lurched to my feet, sucked in air, and leaped over the side.

I hit the water headfirst, sliced in and under. As I sank, I curled myself into a tight ball, dragged my cuffed wrists under my buttocks and up in front of me. I'd almost come down on Shev's back. He twisted around. I saw the rubber bag at his belt, filled with the money he'd found. Saw his startled face behind the glass mask. Then he was trying to bring around his speargun to fire it at me.

I dodged the pointed barb, scissored my legs and drove myself against his chest. Reached down with both cuffed together hands and pulled the float knife from his belt scabbard. Shev twisted away from me. My swimming couldn't match his, with those fins aiding him. I made one desperate slash with the knife, hampered by the dragging weight of the water and the awkwardness of the chain linking my wrists. He dodged backwards, but not quickly enough or far enough. The point of the knife slit his throat. Blood shot out to stain the water. His teeth opened and the mouthpiece floated from his lips. I made a fast grab with both hands for the still-loaded speargun as he let go of it. The next instant I was popping up above the surface, gasping for air.

There was the double roar of two simultaneous shots from

Mungo and Frenchy standing at the starboard rail of the boat. Only the rolling of the boat and my own motion in the surface swell saved me. The slugs splashed water on either side of my face.

I dragged in air and dove back down, passing Shev's limp body floating upward to the surface. I dove deep, hanging onto the speargun with my hands and driving myself under the bottom of Mungo's cruiser with my legs.

I came up on the portside, at the ladder. Frenchy turned to the rail above me, looked down and saw me. He was bringing his gun around to aim when I raised the gas-powered speargun and fired it. The short spear flashed upward. Its wide, heavy barb harpooned Frenchy in the stomach, vanished inside <u>him</u>, taking a <u>third</u> of the shaft in after it.

Frenchy let go of his gun and staggered backwards, his face tilted upward for his last stare at the sky. His hands fumbled at the spear shaft sticking out of him. Then his arms fell and his big body toppled over stiffly.

I dropped the empty speargun and grabbed the ladder, climbed the rungs cautiously, ready to let myself fall back in the water. I raised my head over the gunwale. Just enough to see Mungo in the stern waiting for me with his .38 ready.

But then, as abruptly as an explosion, Gronsky shoved himself away from the opposite gunwale and rolled on the deck, revealing that he'd managed to cut his hands loose with the razor blade. Mungo spun away from me to shoot Gronsky. I jumped the rail and started for Mungo.

Mungo hesitated, caught between the two of us, trying to decide which was the most danger to him. The hesitation was fatal. Gronsky stretched out a long arm, snatched up Frenchy's fallen Magnum. It roared and recoiled in his hand. Twice. The heavy slugs slammed into Mungo, hurled him against me. He slid to the deck before I could get a hold on him.

I knelt beside him quickly. He had his eyes squeezed shut against the pain.

I saw the blood welling from the hole in the center of his chest and the one in his abdomen, and knew he was going to die.

I looked away from him. Gronsky was sitting on the deck of the cockpit, looking pleased with himself. Gretchen cowered in the fishing chair to which she was bound. Larry Score lay sprawled with his head propped against the gunwale. He watched me with slitted eyes, clutching his bleeding and shattered shoulder, too sick with pain to move.

I turned back to Mungo. His eyes had opened. He stared up at me without expression. The pain was ebbing from him, the numb cold creeping in to take its place. There wasn't much time.

I hurried into the wheelhouse. Got a pencil and tore a large scrap off the chart of Biscayne Bay. Turning the scrap over, I wrote on it quickly: "I, Al Mungo, swear Larry Score killed Maria Barreto and Daniel Yale on orders from me."

Mungo's eyes were still open when I knelt beside him again. There was still life in him; maybe enough. "Mungo, can you hear me?"

"I—hear—you—rat." His voice was a whisper oozing through clenched teeth.

"*I'm* not the rat," I told him. "Score is. He's the one that played you for a sucker and got you into this."

Mungo said nothing.

"Maybe you're still not quite sure of that," I said. I looked around. "Gronsky, squeeze Score a little."

Gronsky put down the gun and started pulling himself over the deck toward Score, dragging the cast-encased leg behind him. Fear contorted Score's features and fought against his immobilizing pain. He scrambled up on his knees. The arm dangling from the smashed shoulder swung like a pendulum, causing a fresh burst of pain that almost knocked him down on his face. He grabbed the dangling right arm with his left hand, staggered to his feet.

Gronsky's hand reached out and seized his ankle, dragged him back. Score let go of his arm, dug into his pocket and whipped out his knife. The switchblade flicked out and he twisted around to slash at Gronsky's eyes. Gronsky flinched. The point of the knife traced a <u>thin</u> red line the length of his cheek. Then he had hold of Score's wrist. A sharp twist and the knife sprang from Score's limp fingers. Gronsky dragged Score down with him. The fingers of both hands went around Score's neck, completely encircling it, sinking in.

Score flopped and fought like a hooked fish. The fingers sank in deeper. Score's face became suffused with trapped blood, his eyes swelled from their sockets—till he began to look the way Maria Barreto had looked after he'd strangled her. His futile struggles became weaker, weaker . . .

"Easy now," I warned Gronsky.

Gronsky nodded, loosened his grip on Score's throat a bit. Score opened his mouth wide, gasping in air.

"You get *one* chance to tell the truth," I told him. "Just one. Did you kill Sondra Lomax?"

He clawed at Gronsky's strangling fingers with his left hand, not answering.

I said, "Goodbye, Larry." And then, "Go ahead, Gronsky." Gronsky's fingers began to tighten again. "Wait!" Score screeched, his voice forcing out high-pitched through the pressure of Gronsky's hands. "I *did it!* I killed her!"

As a confession, it wouldn't have been worth anything legally even if I'd had the governor of Florida there to hear it. But it had another purpose to serve. I told Gronsky to let go of Score, turned back to Mungo. "Did you hear him?"

"Yeah . . . ." It came out of Mungo like a sigh, barely audible.

"Then you know. He suckered you into all of this. You're going to die, Mungo. You'll be dead before I can possibly get you to a hospital in Miami. But there's one way you can pay him back. Sign this confession that Score did the Barreto and Yale kills for you."

Mungo's hand groped blindly for the pencil in my hand. I put the confession down on the deck beside him, rolled him over on his side, got the pencil in his hand. He couldn't do anything with it unaided. I wrapped my hand around his, helped him to scrawl his name at the bottom of the confession.

As a signature, it was pretty sloppy. But I had Gretchen as my witness that it *was* Mungo's signature. And she was the best possible kind of witness. Thirty million dollars' worth of witness.

I let Mungo down on his back, stood up with the scrap of paper in my hand. Striding across the cockpit, I picked up the razor blade from where Gronsky had dropped it. I went to Gretchen Forrest and cut her loose from the chair. She didn't move. She sat there as though she were still tied, the shock of the fact that she was not a murderess still registering on her.

"You heard Mungo say earlier that he ordered Score to kill Maria Barreto and Danny Yale," I said to her. "And you saw him sign this confession." I picked up one of her hands, stuck the scrap of paper in it and forced her fingers closed around it. "Hold onto this for me."

I turned away from her, went to the starboard gunwale—ready to dive over and get the bag of money from Shev's body.

But I'd taken too much time getting around to it.

As I reached the rail, I saw a shark appear, attracted by Shev's blood, just below the surface where Shev's body floated. The next second the shark's monstrous mouth opened wide, and its teeth clamped shut on Shev's legs.

Then the shark was speeding away from the boat, with Shev's torso projecting sideways from the vise of its jaws. Five hundred yards from the boat, the shark dove, taking Shev down with it, heading for some quiet place in the depths to finish its meal. My shoulders sagged. Something went out of me. A hundred and sixty-seven thousand dollars. I turned dejectedly from the gunwale—and saw that Gronsky was still holding Larry Score by the throat.

"For crissake!" I growled. "Let him go."

Gronsky grinned at me and said, "Sure thing." He took his hands from Score's neck.

Score rolled off Gronsky's cast and flopped on his back on the deck. His eyes and mouth were open. But he didn't move again, and no sound came out of him.

I went to one knee beside Score. Felt his chest with my hands. Looked at Gronsky. "He's dead."

"Wha'd'ya know!" the Mad Russian said cheerfully. "I musta squeezed him a little too hard. Ain't that a shame."

Mungo surprised me. He took much longer at dying than I'd expected. But the end result was as I'd predicted. He'd finished with his dying by the time I docked his boat at the Municipal Pier in Miami.

26.

THE DISTRICT ATTORNEY DIDN'T LIKE IT. Miami Homicide didn't like it. The sheriff's office didn't like it.

My statement of the facts and Mungo's scribbled deathbed confession didn't make them like it anymore.

But then Gretchen Forrest backed me up, right down the line. A restored Gretchen Forrest, with all the arrogant confidence of thirty million inherited dollars in her manner and voice. And with her attorney—who happened to be an ex-governor of the state—lending the full support of his considerable political weight.

The D.A. and the sheriff and Homicide decided to swallow it—whether they liked it or not.

They formally charged the deaths of Maria Barreto and Danny Yale to Mungo and Score—getting Gronsky and me off the hook. It wasn't anything they could have proved to a jury. But with Mungo and Score both dead, they could issue the statement without tackling the embarrassing problem of making a case in court.

I didn't bring up the subject of Sondra Lomax, and Gretchen followed my lead. There'd have been no way of proving Score had murdered Sondra, and Score had already paid for it, anyway.

Gretchen Forrest made no objection when I held her to the letter of our agreement. She paid me the three-thousand-dollar bonus for getting the problem of Sondra Lomax off her back, and freeing her from the possibility of unfavorable publicity. Together with the fifteen hundred I got for Gronsky's ring, that made forty-five hundred dollars. I gave five hundred of it back to Gronsky to help with his hospital bills. That left me four thousand.

I took the four thousand dollars and Kit Forrest across the Gulf Stream in my boat to play the roulette wheel in Nassau.

We were there together for a week. It was fine—except that Kit hit a winning streak at the wheel, and I ran into a losing streak. At the end of the week, a yachtful of Kit's friends came along, and she went off to Havana with them. She invited me to come along, but by then I was flat broke.

That's the way it goes.

The rich get richer, and private eyes go back to work to earn another stake.

Six months later, I received an engraved invitation to attend Kit's marriage to a stockbroker in New York. I didn't go. I bought a little bronze statue of a racing horse and sent it to her as a wedding present.

ABOUT THE AUTHOR

Marvin H. Albert was the author of more than a hundred books, from westerns, mysteries, and spy novels, to works of history, including "The Long White Road," a biography of the Antarctic explorer Ernest Shackleton.

Revered in France as a master of detective fiction, he wrote under many pseudonyms, including Nick Quarry, Al Conroy, Ian McAllister and Mike Barone. Ten of his books were adapted into feature films, including two of the Tony Rome novels.

His acclaimed *Stone Angel* series, written while living in France during the latter part of his life, featured French-American detective Pete Sawyer. He died in 1996.

1.

THE ROOM SMELLED OF BLOOD. There was a drying crust of it along one corner of Lou Kovac's gasping mouth, half a bottle of it hanging over his bed, and more of it dripping through the transparent plastic tube running from the bottle to the needle stuck in the vein of his left arm. The arm was still muscular, but its hairs were gray, almost white. With a sense of shock it came to me that I'd known Lou for so long that I hadn't been aware of his growing old.

The beating had abruptly completed his aging process, as effectively as a wrecking crew ripping out the interior supports of a condemned building.

It was an old man who lay on the bed, fighting for what was left of his life. He panted for each breath. The tortured heaving of his chest under the sheet was weak and uncertain. He fought for his life unknowingly, drugged into oblivion by injections of morphine which had separated his conscious mind from his agony.

The nurse was glaring at me from across the bed and pressing hard at the call button. I ignored her, moving to the edge of the bed.

Whoever had administered the beating had concentrated on him from the shoulders down. His face was unmarked. But it was a cruel caricature of the face I'd known. Where its bone structure had been prominent it now stood out in stark ridges; where the flesh had been taut, it was shrunken. The skin of his bald head and gaunted face was splotchy gray, his lips like dirty wax. His closed eyelids lay flat, as though his eyes had retreated deep into their sockets to escape what had been done to him.

Whatever they'd beaten him with—baseball bats was the best guess—had been used with systematic savagery.

They'd smashed both his kneecaps and his right hip, shattered his rib cage. His broken hands lay on either side of him on the sheet, held in complicated structures of wired splints.

The damage done to his stomach, kidneys and other organs was so severe that it had taken two surgeons over an hour to stop his internal bleeding, before they could begin work on his shattered bones.

I was staring down at him frozenly when a doctor bustled into the surgery recovery room.

"What are you doing here?" he snapped at me. "No one other than hospital staff is allowed in this room."

The nurse on the other side of Lou's bed said quickly, "I told him that, doctor."

"She told me," I acknowledged, not looking up.

"Then what are you doing in here?" he demanded.

"I'm his friend," I said tonelessly. "I came to see for myself."

"I don't care who you are, you have no business being in this room. He's in no condition

"What is his condition?" I raised my head and turned it and looked at the doctor. "Will he live?"

He met my eyes and some of the indignation leaked out of him. "Yes—he'll live. That is . . . ." The doctor tore his eyes from mine and looked at the man on the bed. "He's going to live. But at this moment, and considering his age, I can't say what he'll be like for the rest of his life. After what Mr. Kovac has been through, you see."

"I do see," I told him. "Thank you." I walked past him and went through the door.

Outside in the corridor I leaned the backs of my shoulders

against the wall and fumbled a Lucky from my pocket. I got it lit and sucked my lungs full of smoke. After a time I let the smoke out, slow. When the cigarette was down to a stub, I crushed it under and went to see Art Santini at Homicide.

Lieutenant Santini was behind the desk in his small gray office at headquarters when I entered, filling out a case report with a red ballpoint pen. He was a plump man with a round, deceptively bland face. As I closed his door, he raised his head and stuck the end of the pen between his even white teeth, leaning back in his chair. His dark liquid eyes watched me lower myself onto the other chair, between the filing cabinets and his desk. We looked at each other.

Santini put the pen down on the unfinished report.

"They let you see him, Rome?"

"I saw him." I got out a cigarette and rolled it between my fingers. Then I broke it in half and threw it into his wastebasket. "You'll be yanked off the case," I told him. "Lou's going to live. So it's not murder, or even manslaughter."

"There's still attempted murder," Santini pointed out,

"Not even that. Assault and battery. They didn't intend to kill him. They did what they set out to do. Not more. Not less. They knew how. Professional goons."

Santini nodded. "Uh-huh. How come? What was he doing that'd get him that kind of attention?"

"I don't know," I said. "I hoped you could tell me."

"Well, I can't. We went over his office and apartment real careful. There wasn't a thing to tell us what he'd been working on lately. I guess we'll have to wait and find out what gives from Kovac himself, when he comes around enough."

"Don't count on that," I said softly. "It'll be a helluva long time before Lou's in any shape to talk. Even then, he may not remember anything. A working over like he got doesn't usually leave a man much to go on with. Even money he'll be doing the rest of his living in a nursing home."

I stared bitterly at the dusk shimmering in the fat shaft of

Florida sunlight that lanced through the single window of Santini's office. "He's an old man, did you know that? Too old to be playing tag with hoods."

"Yeah," Santini said. "He's been around a long time. Used to be on the force back in the old days, before he shifted to private detective work."

I nodded. "He was my father's best friend. They started as rookies together. When I was born, Lou was made my godfather. When I quit the department, he helped me get my private detective license."

"I know," Santini said. "That's why I called, you. Kovac hasn't got any close kin around, has he?"

"Nobody." I stared back into the hot sunlight streaming through the window. Then I looked at Santini. "All right. What have you got on it so far? Anything?"

Santini sighed. "Damn little. Some woman who wouldn't identify herself phoned in and said she'd heard what sounded like somebody getting beaten up in the alley next to the building where Kovac has his office. By the time a prowl car got there, Kovac was all by himself in the alley. The guys who'd done the wrecking job on him were gone. We haven't turned up anybody so far who saw them."

"And that's it? Nothing more?"

"There's one thing." Santini hesitated. "It may not mean anything, though."

"Tell me."

"We found a motel receipt in Kovac's wallet. He was paid up for a full week in advance. The week still has three days to go. A place called the Seaview Motel—in Coffin City."

I knew of Coffin City, an ironic name for a city. Its founder had been John Coffin but lately the name had a less pleasant identification. It had a number of reputations. Most long-standing was its reputation as a distribution center for moonshine turned out by illegal stills hidden away in the Everglades and Big Cypress Swamp. Since the war Coffin City had also acquired a reputation as an anything-goes tourist trap. Still more recently, it had been experiencing a building boom in home developments for retired couples.

"Of course," Santini said, "it may not mean he was working on a case. Maybe he just went there for a vacation."

"Coffin City's not the kind of place Lou'd pick for a holiday. And if he went there for time off, why was he back in Miami, with three paid-up days still to go at this Seaview Motel?"

"I wondered about it," Santini admitted. "So I made a call first thing this morning to the police chief in Coffin City. Man named Hollis Cobb. He said he didn't know anything about any private detective named Lou Kovac. But he promised to ask around and find out if Kovac was working on a job of some kind there." Santini paused and looked at me. "Which he may do. Or he may not."

I narrowed my eyes at Santini. "Meaning which?"

"Meaning he'll do it if it suits him to. He won't if he's got any reason to hush anything up. I also made another call this morning. To the State Police. According to the cop I talked to, this Police Chief Hollis Cobb is deep in the pocket of Hugh Tallant, the guy who runs the moonshining and everything else that's below-board around Coffin City."

"That's interesting," I said slowly, thinking about it.

"Could be. Or it could be a wrong guess."

"Yeah." I stood up suddenly and headed for the door. When I got it open, I looked back at Santini.

"I'll be in touch—just in case you dig up anything more. You are going to keep digging into what happened to Lou, aren't you?"

"Sure," Santini said, not hopefully. "But you know how hard it is to nail down any of these professional jobs. The bastards that did this may never be found."

"This time they'll be found," I told Santini, very quietly. "You lay any odds you want on it. They'll be found."

I went down to my Olds and drove away. I considered paying a visit to Lou Kovac's office and apartment. But it would have been wasted motion. Art Santini had been to both places. He was too much of a cop to have missed anything.

Instead, I drove south out of Miami to Dinner Key, and walked out along the pier to the Straight Pass, a cabin cruiser that served as my home. I got the bottle out of the galley and sat for a time in the cockpit fishing chair, sipping brandy and thinking about Lou Kovac—and Coffin City.

Tangerine, a battle-scarred waterfront tomcat who knew me for a soft touch, prowled down the pier and sprang into the cockpit and eyed me fiercely. After a while I got him a saucer of milk. While he lapped it greedily, I went back to sipping brandy in the fishing chair and thinking.

Tangerine finished the milk, gave me a glare that passed for a look of gratitude in his circle, and stalked off along the Dinner Key dock in search of more handouts. I watched till he was out of sight near the big luxury yachts along the first pier. Then I went into the cabin and began getting things out of the locker and stowing them in a suitcase.

The final item I took from the locker was the box containing my newly acquired Luger automatic.

I'd acquired the Luger the same way I'd come by the boat: I'd won it in a craps game. I'd only had the Luger pistol two weeks, but of all the weapons I'd ever used, it was my favorite.

I'd sailed out on the Gulf Stream and done some target practice with it against floating objects. The Luger had lived up to its reputation, fitting my hand so naturally. That it seemed to aim itself. All I'd had to do was point it at a target, as easily as I'd point my finger. What the Luger was pointed at, it hit.

I loaded it and slipped it into its soft kid holster and hooked the holster to my belt under my jacket. Putting two extra clips of ammo in under my shirts, I closed the suitcase, carried it with me back to my car, and drove north to Coffin City.